The Washington Academy of Sciences was incorporated in 1898 as an affiliation of eight Washington D.C. area scientific societies. The founders included Alexander Graham Bell and Samuel Langley, Secretary of the Smithsonian Institution. Then as now, the purpose of the new Academy is to encourage the advancement of science and "to conduct, endow, or assist investigation in any department of science."

Over the past decade the publishing industry has undergone dramatic changes. The old, proud publishing houses have, for the most part, become virtually indistinguishable from other commercial establishments, delegating their traditional editorial functions to agents whose primary purpose is to meet the demands of the market. Increasingly, authors are eschewing the agent-to-publisher-to-mass market route and are turning to on-demand, self- publishing. Whether the process includes a traditional publisher or not, editorial niceties and fact-checking often have no place in the process.

This has led to a number of problems, the worst of which is – from the Academy's point of view –the great increase in "junk science" being published both as fiction and non-fiction. The Academy therefore offers those Academy members who have written a science-heavy book, the opportunity to submit the book to our editors for review *of the science therein.* The manuscript receives the same rigorous scientific review that we accord articles published in our Journal. If the reviewer(s) determine(s) that the science is accurate, the author may then continue the publishing process of choice and the book may display the seal of The Washington Academy of Sciences. In cases where the Academy editors determine that the book is scientifically accurate but requires editing, they may return the manuscript to the author and request that it be satisfactorily edited.

BLOOD WILL SNITCH

a Bea Goode mystery

Peg Kay
with Michael Coble, PhD.

WASHINGTON ACADEMY OF SCIENCES

Acknowledgments

This book was a lot of fun to write. Unlike its three predecessors, it poked its literary nose into a bevy of nooks and crannies. Because of that, I needed lots of help and in the course of garnering that help I conferred with a number of terrific people I might never have met otherwise.

The people who filled me in on the DC Jazz scene and the Shaw neighborhood in the 1990's:

Saleem Hylton of the African American Music Association, Washington, DC. introduced me to the Black music scene in 1993.

Anne Rowlins, super-volunteer at the DC Historical Society

Rusty Hassan, jazz jockey at WPFW, who furthered my education on Black Music and the scene in DC's Shaw District as it was in 1993, as well as

The Staff at Shaw Main Streets and

Bill Brower, DC's guru of jazz history.

David Harp, a wonderful wildlife photographer, described Bloodsworth Island and the challenge of photographing the Heron Rookeries.

Dr. Mark Holland and Dr. Gene Williams, of Salisbury University, told me what I needed to know about plant biology and beyond.

Mindy Suchinsky of the law firm, West & Feinberg, led me through the intricacies of estate law

BLOOD WILL SNITCH

Jo Johnson, Director of Arlington Virginia's Crisis Intervention Center explained the traumatic effect of rape.

Father Frank Haig ushered me through the Catholic Rites of Marriage

Jim Reid, my neighbor and the son of an old time cop and Captain James Bartlett of the Alexandria Police Force kept me from making a fool of myself law-enforcement-wise.

And, of course, the folk who watch my p's, q's, and commas:

Danielle Briggs; the Northern Virginia Writers Guild, led by Ashok Shenolikar; and as always, Molly Cameron.

You'd think with all of that assistance, Blood Will Snitch would have no flaws. Not at all. I'm sure I've managed to sneak in a few of my own.

Cover design by Emily Yahn

CAST OF CHARACTERS

The Crew from LIT

Beatrice (Bea) Goode: The narrator. Member of the Director's staff, Federal
        Laboratory of Industrial Technology (LIT)

Alex Carfil: Bea's husband. Director of the Computer Sciences Center

Dr. P.I. Lee (Pie): LIT's Director

Don Cromarty: Member of the Director's staff

Dr. Molly Cameron: Director of the Biology Center

Jeanne Cameron: Member of Bea's staff (no relation to Molly)

Jim Daly: Member of Bea's staff

Marge Dunn: Member of Bea's staff

Ben Goldfarb: Member of Bea's staff – shared with Don Cromarty

Lenore: LIT's Departmental secretary

Chrissie Daly : Daughter of Jim Daly, intern in the Biology Center

Ralph Manley : Horticulturist in the Biology Center and mentor to Chrissie Daly

Dr. Elizabeth (Bessie) Lee: Pie's wife

Dr. Adrienne Hodler: Scientist in the Biology Center

Miriam Manley: Ralph's wife

Blake Halonen: An intern in the Biology Center

The Group from the Forensic Lab

Paul Richards: Director of the Forensic Lab within the Department of Justice

Cody Kletsch: Supervisor of Team 3

Elliott Giles: Team 3 Technician

Jasmine (Jazz) Nishiyama: Team 3 Analyst

Rep. Jimboy Davies: Member of the Congressional Authorization Committee

Jimboy Davies, Junior: Congressman Jimboy Davies' son

Yvonne Danielson: Team 3 Technician

The Folk from the Farm

Daryl and Claudia Coker: Owners of an alpaca farm and Bea's and Alex's
        weekend cabin on the farm

Daryl Jr. And Sandy Coker: Son and Daughter-in-Law of the Cokers

Gertie the Alpaca and Louise the Llama

BLOOD WILL SNITCH

The Music Makers

Lomas Hopper: Bass player

Arthur Burbank: Drummer

Willis Rockwell: Sax player

Glenna and Al: Members of the audience

Michelle Rockwell: Willis's wife

Florence Barney:Couturier

The Citizens of Bella Villa

Chuck Hadaman: Facilities manager of the Department of Trade and Industry and
        Bea's, Alex's and Ben's friend

Walt Avery: Sheriff's deputy

Joe: Another deputy

Petey Petrofsky: A mentally handicapped 12-year old

Claude and Midge Petrofsky: Petey's parents

Sam: Sheriff of Bella Villa County

Pudge: The hospital administrator

Father Haydn: Priest at St. Michaels

Duane: Proprietor of The Rabbit Hole

Charity Nesbitt: The frump

Dexter Hamilton: Manager of Cabot House

The Residents of Alexandria

The sonuvabitch

Johnny Notte: Next door neighbor of Alex and Bea and member of the Mafia

Marilyn Notte: Johnny's wife

Cop with the Squad Car

Mrs. Brattice

Howard Brattice

Brat Brattice

Buddy the Grocer

2 cops on the Lawn

Chief Reddy of the Alexandria Police

> And a cameo appearance by Freddy Langsteth of the
> Office of Managment and Budget

PROLOGUE

Autumn 1986

The solo sailor found the Chesapeake in fine shape. A nice breeze ruffled the water and kept the sail full. The sun was high but intermittently covered by clouds, preventing the day from becoming uncomfortably hot. The sailor was a pleasant looking man, lean and fit, in his early fifties. Aside from a touch of heartburn, he felt at the top of his game.

He could have easily afforded a bigger, faster, fancier boat but he loved his little dinghy. It had been with him a long time. He grinned to himself. "A poor thing, but mine own."

He raised his head in boisterous song.

"The officers ride in their whaleboat,
   The admiral rides in his barge,
   It doesn't go a little bit faster,
   But, it makes the old bast...."

The sailor suddenly felt as if he had been hit by a Mack truck. He grabbed his chest. He had just time to think, "So this is what a heart attack feels like."

He was dead before he hit the deck.

CHAPTER 1

May 19, 1993

We dumped the breakfast dishes into the dishwasher, grabbed our spring jackets and beat it out the door and into a light drizzle.

Alex slid into the passenger seat. "Think it'll clear by the end of the day?"

"Supposed to. It'd be nice to drive home with the top down."

"Do you have a start line?" I asked.

"I do, indeed. What can you do with this? *A fat acrobat named Louise,*"

"Sheesh. Do you want to go out for dinner tonight?"

Alex shot me The Look. "Don't change the subject."

"Oh, alright. Let me think."

"So think, awready."

"Okay. Here. *Was arrested while on a trapeze,*"

"How could she get arrested while she was on a trapeze?" Alex asked. "Cops don't fly on trapezes."

"That's your problem. Solve it."

Silence, then *"For daring to bare her rump in the air.* Ball's in your court, m'dear."

"Hmmm. Hah! *And floating spare parts in the breeze."*

I can explain all that. Alex, my husband of some two years,

and I work for LIT, the Laboratory for Industrial Technology, which is subservient to the Department of Trade and Industry, (DoTI, pronounced "dotty" – and yes, it is). Alex is Chief of the Computer Sciences Center. (LIT's other Center is BiologicalSciences). I'm a Management Scientist in the Director's Office. Alex and I week-end in a log cabin on an alpaca farm near the little town of Bella Villa. The cabin is a short commute to the LIT office, just up a winding road in a mostly-rural part of Maryland. This minor commute happens in the evening on Friday and in the morning on Monday. The rest of the week we make the long commute to and from Alexandria, Virginia where we have our real house. Every once in a while we consider moving to Bella Villa. But it would be ludicrous to have a house in Bella Villa and a week-end cabin only a mile away.

The alpaca farm is located between our Alexandria home and LIT. Every day we would drive by the pasture where the alpacas hang out. After a while, we began stopping there and treating them to apple slices. Daryl Coker, the farmer, observed this unlikely behavior and one day he intercepted us. We exchanged introductions. The next day, he met us again, and told us that he had a little cabin on his property. His son and daughter-in-law had lived there until they had enough money to buy a home of their own. The cabin stood empty and the Cokers didn't like that. We could have it rent-free if we would pay for the utilities and maintenance. After exchanging references, we inspected the cabin and the deal was struck. We have grown to love that little cabin, the alpacas, the llamas that guard them, and the Cokers.

As for the house in Alexandria – we love that house, too. We love being able to walk out the front door and into a city, with its restaurants, its theater, its whole ambiance. So should we move closer to LIT? Nah. We'll keep both the cabin and the long commute.

And this is where the limericks enter. Much of the long commute is lovely. But a body can take just so much lovely and then it gets boring. For about a year we entertained ourselves by warbling Gilbert and Sullivan, but even G&S palls over time – particularly when the warblers are Alex and me. So we began to consider other ways to amuse ourselves on the trek northward. And we recalled Bobby Figgle and his limericks at the Army Observatory.[1] So, starting from there, we developed an advanced version of the limerick thing. One of us initiates the limerick with a single line. The other adds a second line. The initiator then puts in the two middle lines. And the other of us winds it up. Needless to say, the limerick must scan. So far, the limericks have indeed scanned, so the penalty for not scanning has not yet been determined. Pushing the culprit out of the moving Mustang might be a bit excessive.

Alex pulled the car into our parking slot. As is often the case, the space was surrounded by a group of techies plus Don, the other member of the Director's staff. They were awaiting the day's limerick.

"Yo," Alex called.

> *"A fat acrobat named Louise*
> *Was arrested while on a trapeze*

---

[1] See *The Case of the Eclipsed Astronomer*

For daring to bare
Her rump in the air
And floating spare parts in the breeze."

There were a few minutes wait while the group decided whether the effort deserved cheers or boos and catcalls. Cheers won and, gratified, Alex went off to the CompSci Center while Don and I headed to the administration wing.

Don Cromarty and I staff the Director's office. Internal stuff, such as Congressional visits, publications, personnel problems, and anything else that occurs to the Director is handled by me and my staff.

Don is the budget guy and the designated meeting-goer. The Federal government holds lots of meetings. For example, LIT's representative attends those meetings that decide which products the government will get behind when a company wants to expand foreign markets. Easier to give an example than to explain. A recent meeting discussed three products: a self steering bicycle, a pharmaceutical product to fight the common cold, and an artificial intelligence based telephone call-screener. Each product had its advocate and after listening to the arguments, the committee decided which product our embassies would push. Don was LIT's representative to the committee, there to describe the pros and cons of pushing the call-screener.

When I joined the agency, he was serving as deputy to the previous LIT director. I reported to him. Once Pie became director, Don lobbied successfully to get me promoted to the Director's staff. Don remained the designated meeting goer since he has a technical background while I have some difficulty coping with an advanced-model microwave. Don had been a good boss and was now a good colleague. I wouldn't say that he's sensitive, in the way that Alex is sensitive. That is, Don doesn't intuitively know when someone needs a hug. But he's kind; he's fair; and if he recognizes that you're having a problem, he tries to help. He's a big, shambling guy with a moon face and a light-up-the-sky grin.

Alex and I have become good friends of Don and his wife, Connie, although we don't see as much of them now as we normally do. They are remodeling their house. Extensively.

Don and Connie have two kids. Twins, they are in their first year of college -- Linda at the Naval Academy, Larry at the Coast Guard Academy.

Between the remodeling and Don's passion for playing softball and coaching a Little League team, he doesn't have much time for socializing.

Walking down the admin corridor, Don described the remodeling crisis-of-the-moment.

"Oh, man. This was a beaut. They had finished installing the joists and putting up the drywall in the new family room .... You know where our laundry tubs are?"

"Uh uh."

"They're in the basement close to where that dry wall is. There's kind of a crawl space above the family room. The contractor was supposed to close the space off but he didn't. Well, our cat jumped up on the laundry tub and then up into the crawl space and fell down between the dry wall and the basement wall. When Connie and I came home one of those morons was standing on a ladder lowering a strip of carpet into the space where the cat is. He was trying to convince the cat to climb up the carpet. The other guys were standing around giving him advice."

I broke up.

"It's not funny, dammit."

I stopped laughing except for an occasional choking noise. "Did they get the cat out?"

"Connie told them that the cat was unlikely to oblige and they'd have to find another way to rescue her."

"They tell Connie that they'll come back tomorrow and do it. Connie went postal. She screamed at them that they either got the cat out now or not to come back ever. We'd get someone else to finish the job and they could whistle Dixie for their money.

"So they went back into the family room and cut a hole in the new drywall. And there's the cat. Except the joists are close together and she can't get her head through to come out."

"Is she still there?"

"Of course not. They had to chip a little bit off near the bottom of each of the two joists to make a space big enough for her head. They'll have to replace the joists and the drywall. Anyway, the cat got out and she was mad as hell. Wouldn't have anything to do with us until it was time for her dinner."

I commiserated appropriately and peeled off to my office to begin my working day – as usual, by answering the phone. Congressman Bowlden's admin assistant wanted us to set up a tour of LIT for a constituent. A Very Important Constituent. And in case I missed it, A Very *Very* Important Constituent.

"What's the guy most interested in?" I asked.

"The biology technology. He's an agri-business type."

Ouch. Molly Cameron, the BioCenter's Chief, does not like her lab disturbed. "When does he want to come?"

"Day after tomorrow. I'll send you briefing notes." He hung up, leaving me to stare at the receiver.

I leaned back in my chair and wondered how I was going to tell Molly about the upcoming visitation. Should I take the off-hand approach? "By the way Molly, Congressman Bowden's constituent is going to drop in on you. He's a nice guy." Should I come all over Director's Office? "Molly, expect a constituent of Congressman Bowden to be in your office the day after tomorrow. Please prepare your staff." Maybe I should grovel. "I hate to ask this, Molly, but...."

I sighed, stood up, and walked over to the Director's office. If I looked sufficiently pitiful, maybe he'd agree to give the good news to Molly.

The Federal government, like most large enterprises, assigns office space based on the importance of the occupant. Thus, our Director was rattling around in a corner space the size of a small amphitheater, with a magnificent view of the parking lot. It was a pleasant office, befitting his exalted station. It contained a largish mahogany desk behind which the Director could put his tush on a comfortable swivel chair. There was a sofa and a couple of easy chairs. The center of the room was occupied by a small conference table, around which were six less imposing chairs. A bookcase stood against one wall. It contained various volumes related to the governance of the Federal government, a few unread volumes on how to manage whatever, and some copies of the *Journal of*

Microbiology, the *Journal of Microbiological Methods*, the *Journal of Microbiology and Biotechnology*, the *Journal of Microbiology and Biology Education*, and for good measure, Julia Child's *Mastering the Art of French Cooking*. You gotta love that guy.

Pie was hanging up his phone as I walked in. The eminent Dr. P.I. Lee was brought to LIT by the former Secretary of DoTI and persuaded to stay on by the current Secretary. Since Pie loves his job, it didn't take much persuading. His initial appointment came as a gratifying surprise to me. My first (deceased) husband Harry and I were honorary niece and nephew to Uncle Pie and Aunt Bessie. And now I had him for a boss. What more could a poor working girl ask?

As you many have gathered, Pie's a microbiologist. He came to LIT from MIT where he had the title of Distinguished Professor. He is a most elegant gentleman, the product of a Chinese mathematician father and a Jewish housewife mother. Pie's hair is always stylishly cut and brushed to a sheen. His trousers are sharply creased. His shoes are burnished. And he has a perfectly ridiculous Brooklyn accent.

"Good morning, *bubeleh*. I'm glad you're here. That was Molly Cameron on the phone. I was about to call you. She wants a favor from us. From you in particular. She'll be here in a minute."

The gods smile upon me. I'll do whatever the woman asks as long as she makes nice to the Congressman's constituent.

The door opened and Molly entered. "Bea, I have a huge favor to ask. It's okay if you say no."

"First let *me* beg a favor from *you*." I explained about the Very *Very* Important Constituent and the fact that the Congressman was on our Authorization Committee.

"You want me to pretend that I'm glad he's disrupting my lab."

"Yes."

"Okay. Now can I ask my favor? You can forget about saying no."

Pie and I nodded.

Molly sat down on the couch. "You know the Forensic Lab, just the other side of the Department of Rural Affairs facility down the road?"

"Yeah. Isn't it part of the Justice Department?"

"That's the one. It shouldn't be located in Justice. It should be attached to a university or some other place with a scientific interest. However, it's not the only misplaced object in the Federal government. To get to the point, Paul Richards, the Lab Director is a good friend of mine and he's a worried man. They buy a month's worth of reagents at a time. Reagents are expensive – a month's worth costs maybe $20,000. That's $240,000 a year. The vials are delivered to the lab packed in individual boxes, each box costing about $2,000. And the Lab is running out of them long before the month is up. Can Bea infiltrate the Lab and try to discover who's stealing the stuff?"

"Why me?" I squeaked, momentarily forgetting about the Very *Very* Important Constituent.

"Because," said Molly, "you've been involved in three earlier investigations. Paul heard about them and asked for you. You could pretend to be doing a management audit, whatever that might be."

"I'll do it if it's alright with Pie."

Pie gave his blessing. Rats! I was stuck with it.

As Molly made her way out, Don made his way in, budget spreadsheets in hand. "What brought Molly here?"

Pie and I explained.

Pie turned to me. "What *is* a management audit?"

"It's when someone with a degree, who probably knows nothing about the organization under study, looks at the ways the organization is managed, how it uses its resources, how it does its planning and then makes recommendations about how it can improve."

Pie said, "Is it worth doing?"

"Depends. I was brought in here in the first place to do a management audit but once I was here the Director decided he didn't want to be audited and shelved the whole thing. It might have been worth doing then. Not now."

Pie frowned. "Why not?"

"Because it would only screw things up. The first thing an auditor should do, but rarely does, is look at what the organization is there for, compare its reason for being with the results it gets, and if the results are good – don't fix it. You might want to do a little tinkering around the edges but an outside auditor wouldn't have the faintest idea where to tinker. Do you think someone with no knowledge of the organization would know if too much or too little money was being spent on personnel versus contracts? Only when the results are lousy should the audit continue."

Don grinned. "You wouldn't believe what happened at one of the DRA labs a couple of years ago."

Pie said, "I'd believe anything of the government. Hit me with it."

"Well," said Don, "the Department decided that all of its units should have a management audit – except, of course, the Director's office. So everybody got the audit. Only one unit was deemed unsatisfactory. Those infidels just didn't follow the prescribed procedures for management."

"So *nu?*"

Don went on, "That particular unit had produced three Nobel prize winners within ten years."

I asked, "What did the lab Director do?"

Don laughed. "Said, 'Thank you for your input' and went on churning out Nobelists."

I buzzed the individual members of my staff and asked them to meet me in the small conference room.

It isn't a large staff – one less member and we could probably meet in a phone booth. Jeanne Cameron (no relation to Molly) handles LIT's travel, oversees the support staff, and takes care of routine personnel matters (I get to handle the hot potatoes). She's engaged in a not-too-secret romance with Jim Daly. They don't do any smooching in the office – after all, they're not horny kids. But they *have* been spotted playing footsie in the lunch room. They'll almost certainly get married since while not prudes, they are also not not-prudes. I don't think they'll stay comfortable in a relationship outside the bonds of matrimony.

Jim deals with most Congressional inquiries. I get the call if something Very *Very* Important comes up. Jim also shows visitors –

usually school groups – around. He has a goofy sense of humor. While greeting school groups, he's been known to wear an Albert Einstein mask while speaking in what he claims is an Austrian accent. He's also the sire of Chrissie, an undergraduate intern in Molly Cameron's lab.

Marge Dunn honchos publications. The first thing you notice about Marge is that she's a beautiful woman. Carrot-topped, the merest suggestion of freckles, perfectly proportioned. Once you get past the stunning package, you discover that she's a first-rate editor. Both government and private sector scoundrels keep trying to lure her away from us. But she's married to a retired Microsoft millionaire; she doesn't need money and she loves her job here.

LIT nearly lost her when I tried to give her some help in the form of Ethel the Useless. Ethel resented me from the day I joined the LIT staff. In the scheme of things, the then-director assigned her to my staff. She did not want to be assigned to me. She thought she should have had my job and I should be reporting to her. Fat chance. The woman was a living icon of incompetence. I tried desperately to find something she could do without endangering the agency. An opportunity came when several of our scientists decided to publish papers. The papers all landed on Marge's desk at the same time, overwhelming her. We decided to let Ethel try her hand at editing. Bad choice. She butchered the paper beyond recognition. The authors had a joint hissy. And Marge threatened to quit if I ever let that dumbhead near a publication again. And yes. Marge knew she had agreed to it. So what.

A little, but not much, more about Ethel later.

Half of Ben Goldfarb makes up the last of my staff. The

other half belongs to Don and the arcane world of budget analysis. Ben does international trade statistics with me. He's kind of quirky. His garb, for one thing. Today he was clothed in a spiffy light blue polyester suit, striped orange and green shirt, and a Minnie Mouse tie. For another thing, the man loves statistics. All statistics. Indiscriminately. He can quote baseball statistics, I think back to the days of Abner Doubleday. He can probably quote the number of raindrops that fell in Bangladesh in 1887 as opposed to 1888.

And that's the staff assembled to listen to me tell them of my assignment to the Forensic Lab. "I'll come by LIT every morning before I go over there. Urgent stuff I'll deal with right away. If there's anything that can wait until the morrow, I'll deal with it then. If something important comes up while I'm there, Lenore will have my contact number."

"How long do you think this will take, Bea?" Jeanne asked.

"No idea, but if it goes on for more than two weeks, I'll ask Pie to yank me."

Marge, the compleat editor, said, "Off topic, but did any of you read the article in the Dermatology Journal about eczema?"

"Why would I read an article in the Dermatology Journal?" Jim asked.

"I don't know," Marge said, "I did. I thought you might."

We paused a minute while we wondered why Marge had read it. "So what was in it?" Jeanne inquired.

"A stupid five year long study with an insufficient number of subjects that claimed to 'prove' that childhood eczema was a lifelong problem. It would keep recurring until death. Can you imagine Molly Cameron letting that kind of garbage out of her lab?

And besides that, it read as if it were written by a semi-literate 10-year-old."

Not one of us could imagine either Molly letting it out of her lab or Marge letting it go to press.

Finally, Ben remarked, "There's been a rash of those dermatology studies lately. Kind of gets under your skin."

I forgot to mention that Ben is an inveterate punster. That's why we don't let him deal with the Hill.

Ben walked me back to my office.

"I've got a start on the high tech exports. Counting aerospace, computers, pharmaceuticals, scientific instruments, and electrical machinery, about $91 billion in exports last year. They don't lump biotech into the high tech category but before the decade is out they will, or at least they should. I'll factor it into my report."

"Could you break it down by components? With a smidgeon of analysis if possible."

"Sure. Here's a preview. China's high tech exports are just a mote on the chart now. But watch it. Those guys are hungry and they're using cheap slave labor. They'll catch up with us. I think in the long run, corruption and quality control will knock them back."

"What makes you think so?"

Ben went on. "Just a hunch. People who use slave labor aren't the most savory citizens in the world. And slave labor isn't going to be meticulous about quality. And the slave holders aren't going to be any more meticulous about checking the quality. That's going to hurt their exports.

"India is another place to look out for. They probably won't overtake us, but they'll take a bite out of our exports. I'll concoct a fat analysis before the week is done.

"In another vein – this time no pun intended -- have you seen the latest statistics on AIDS?"

Uh oh. Ben and statistics. "No, Ben, I haven't."

"It's looking like an epidemic. In 1989 there were 90,000 AIDS related deaths in the US. By 1990 the number was 120,000, 156,000 in 1991, and last year 195,000. You watch, by 1995 AIDS will be a leading cause of death for all Americans. We'll be lucky if the death toll doesn't go much over 300,000."

I interjected, "I think AIDS research is high on the Surgeon General's agenda."

"It is," Ben said, "but it isn't all that high on Mr. Clinton's agenda, and if the Surgeon General doesn't keep her mouth shut, she's going to lose her job. Our president is taking the moral high road and he should talk!"

"Don't tell me Bill Clinton is gay."

"No, would that he were. He just beds anyone in a skirt. You know what they said when he was governor of Arkansas?"

"No. What did they say?"

"They said, 'The women in Arkansas are so fast they had to put a governor on them'."

I laughed. "Is there a point to this conversation? Or are we just sitting around schmoozing?"

"I thought you might have seen the AIDS statistics and worried about me."

I nodded. "Had I seen them, I would have."

"Don't worry. I got tested for HIV and I'm clean. So is Chuck Hadaman."

Chuck is Chief of facilities for DoTI. A good friend, he lives in Bella Villa.

Ben went on, "Of all the people who frequent our watering hole, I'm only sure that Chuck, me and one other guy aren't HIV positive."

"Who's the other guy?"

Ben grinned. "Would you believe he's a mafioso? Or whatever they call Italian mobsters."

"In a gay bar? You're putting me on."

"No. For real. He swings both ways. I'm sure his bosses know about it but they're looking the other way. He's married to one of the big guy's daughters. He's gotta stay clean. If he infects his wife her daddy will kill him. Literally."

And with that, Ben departed.

I thought that it might be prudent to get an answer to at least one puzzle before making a fool of myself at the Forensic Lab. In search of Truth, I walked over to the BioCenter, stopped to kibbitz Chrissie and Ralph, her mentor, and knocked on Molly's door.

"Come."

"Hey, Molly, do you have a minute?"

"Maybe a few minutes. Sit down."

I sat. "Why would anyone steal reagents?"

"To sell, of course."

"But who would buy?"

"An impoverished forensic lab, maybe. But more likely, some individual university researchers who don't have the money to buy the reagents retail."

I was not convinced. "And they'd risk buying something that

fell off the back of a truck?"

"Certainly.   If the government wasn't paying for my lab, *I'd* buy it."

And such are the ways of research addicts.

CHAPTER 2

May 20, 1993

I studied my beamish boy across the breakfast table. He really was adorable. From the top of his tousled head through his clear blue eyes and right down to his big toe peeking through the hole in his sock. "Alex," I said, "before you put your shoes on, you might consider changing your socks."

Alex looked down. "Oh, crap," he said. Then brightened. "Well, as long as I have to take my socks off, we might as well take the rest of our clothes off and grab a quick one before we leave for work."

I considered. "Well, we'd have to take a shower..."

Alex had already considered. "If we grab the quick one while we're in the shower we'd save time."

"Brilliant!" I exclaimed. And so it came to pass.

I slid into the drivers seat, turned the key, pulled out, and headed for the office.

"Okay, Alex, try this one. *Punjab grows both wise and brave sons,*"

"Now what's *that* supposed to mean? If I can't think of something, you'd better have a complete limerick to show it's possible."

"And what if I don't?"

Alex thought. "Then I get to pick the place the next time we go out for dinner."

Oh my God. A lifetime of eating chili. "Okay. We needed to define a contingency. But think of the next line anyway."

Alex pondered. "Got it. *Breeds tragedians by the tons.*"

"Tragedians don't get weighed in tons."

Alex hmmphed. "The ones *I* know do."

"You're a hard man, Carfil."

I maneuvered the car out of the neighborhood and onto the freeway.

Alex said, "Stop pretending you need to concentrate on driving and come up with the next lines."

"No sweat. *Though their tragedies glow, Their humor is most low.* Finish it off if you can, buster."

"Do you want to pull off for a snoggle?"

"Alex! Finish it off."

"Oh, okay. *What else can you expect from Puns?*

"Not bad, dearest," I admitted, "Does the limerick scan? It has eight syllables in the first line."

"Same for the second line."

"Six syllables in each of the next lines."

"And another eight to round it off. We're geniuses."

I looked at Alex. "Is that really the plural of genius?"

"I think so. Ask Marge when you get in. She's paid to know things like that."

I pulled into our space in the parking lot, where the welcoming committee awaited.

I stepped from the car and addressed the mob.

"Punjab grows both wise and brave sons,
Breeds tragedians by the tons,
Though their tragedies glow,
Their humor is most low,
What else can you expect from Puns?"

Alex and I waited expectantly while the jury consulted. Bummer. A collective raspberry. The workday had started badly. Early morning, on the other hand, had been quite nifty.

Don and I walked toward our offices.

"What's new on the remodeling front, Don?"

"Oh, boy. They're digging a big hole in the back yard where part of the addition will go. It turns out that the original builder didn't hook the pipes from the bathrooms to any sewer pipes. The water from the bathrooms just emptied into the ground. The guys that are doing my work didn't realize that and didn't notice that the bathroom pipe emptied into the hole they dug. The excavator had barely missed the pipe. So one of the guys was standing in the hole when someone flushed the toilet."

I halted. "You mean..."

Don said, "Yeah, I mean."

I started laughing. Then Don started laughing. We were both standing there laughing helplessly when Lenore approached, with a couple of sheets of paper in hand.

"What's so funny?"

Don and I managed to get ourselves under control. Don told her.

"What's so funny about that?" Lenore asked.

21

Don said, "You had to be there to appreciate it."

Which set me off again.

She waited patiently until I was sentient once more, and handed me the papers. Lenore, a slightly plump, forty-ish woman, is the Director's Office secretary. When I first arrived at LIT she was a supercilious pain in the butt who did not approve of women getting above their appropriate station. In other words, I had a hard time getting the time of day from her. But after Pie became director a couple of years ago, Lenore gradually metamorphosed into a pleasant, helpful, person to have around. I won't say that she became a raging feminist, but at least she didn't mind us girls climbing the departmental ladder. Pie had never said a word to her about her previous attitude. He just came in every day and behaved like Pie, oblivious to the fact that he was setting an example.

I took the papers from her and glanced at them. They were the briefing notes on the Very *Very* Important Constituent. "Dammit!" I said.

"What's wrong?" Lenore asked.

"With the exception of the opening paragraph, this is all about how important the guy is. There doesn't seem to be anything much about the guy himself. He'll be here tomorrow afternoon and I don't have time to research him; I have to get over to the Forensic Lab. Jim, Jeanne, and/or Marge will have to do it."

Lenore said, "Is there anything I can do? I don't know how to do research, but I know most of the support staff at DRA [Department of Rural Affairs] and they can probably fill in some of the blanks."

I looked at Lenore with appreciative awe. "That would be

great. I'll find out who can make time to do the formal research. I'll let you know who to send your findings to. Between you and the rest of the staff we should have a pretty good briefing paper for Pie."

Lenore trundled off to make a start on her assignment. What a miracle Pie had wrought!

I took a poll of the staff. Jim, Jeanne, and Ben were up to their ears in priority tasks. Marge was only up to her chin. She agreed to the assignment and said she'd call Lenore forthwith.

I shuffled through the papers on my desk. Oh, not again! Ethel the Useless was filing yet another EEOC suit in an attempt to get her old job back. She had been a totally miserable employee. She had called a group of mentally disabled kids 'retards'. She had refused to order special airplane meals for an Orthodox Jewish computer scientist. She had edited a BioCenter paper until it was unrecognizable as science. And she had laced my cupcake with ipecac, which she, herself, had inadvertently eaten. The dork couldn't do anything right. The first EEOC suit had been thrown out because we hadn't fired her. We had just conned a sleazy law firm into offering her a job. She took the offer. When the law firm discovered their mistake, they let her go. Now she was re-filing the suit on the grounds that the fact that we had accepted her resignation amounted to discrimination.

Smoke coming out of my ears, I called the personnel department, and got the woman who had sent me Ethel's papers. "What the hell do you want me to do with this rubbish?"

She laughed. "Nothing. We just wanted to hear you squawk."

"Okay, I squawked. Go back to your gin rummy game."

I hung up and walked over to Lenore's desk.

"I forgot to ask you to get me a government car for the duration of my Forensic assignment."

Lenore gave me a smug smile. "I realized that. I've ordered one but I couldn't get it until tomorrow. You'll have to take the Mustang today."

Pie emerged from his office. "Hey, *bubeleh*, Bessie's on her way here for lunch. Do you and Alex want to join us at Hamburgers And?"

"I'll check with Alex, but the provisional answer is 'sure'."

I ducked back into my office and called Alex. 'Sure' it was.

The road to Hamburgers And involves traveling up the mountain a little way, past the Pumpkin Shoot where a man was killed by a flying pumpkin – or squashed, as Ben put it.[2] After that, the road descended past an orchard stand that sold apples and double yolk eggs. The pumpkin shoot and the orchard stand were the only commercial establishments between The Alligator Wrestling emporium and Hamburgers And. While we motored to our lunch destination, Pie at the wheel, I brought them up to date on Don's remodeling follies. Since the Lees had extensively remodeled their house without incident, they found Don's adventures both inexplicable and hilarious. "Where," Bessie asked, between giggles, "did Don find these clowns."

Pie shrugged. "Moe, Curley, and Larry, Inc. in the Yellow Pages."

Which was as good an explanation as we were likely to get.

---

[2] See *The Case of the Eclipsed Astronomer*

Hamburgers And is a loony restaurant located in a strange town. The restaurant offers only hamburgers. The "And" in its name refers to the accessories. You can get your hamburger with onions, tomatoes, lettuce, ketchup, mustard, barbeque sauce, six varieties of cheese, pickles, chili peppers, mayo, slaw, bacon, avocado, fried egg, and mushrooms. All burgers are nine bucks no matter what's on them.

We've never discovered the name of the town. No welcome sign as you enter. The town itself contains a few discouraged stores sprinkled among a bunch of boarded up storefronts. Hamburgers And, the restaurant of choice of the neighboring farms, seems to be its only excuse for existence. I suppose we could find the town's name in the county records, but it's more fun not knowing. Chuck Hadaman keeps promising that he will make an entry sign saying, "Welcome to No Name. Pop. - Who Gives a Damn?"

We ordered our burgers and while we waited, Bessie asked, "Are Jim Daly and Jeanne Cameron planning to get married?"

"Indeed they are," Pie answered.

"What happened to his first wife?" Bessie inquired.

"Sad story," Pie responded. "She died a year or so ago. But she was a religious nut before that. It hadn't been a marriage for a long time. She had moved out of the bedroom claiming that she was the wife of Jesus."

"Why didn't Jim get an annulment on the grounds of psychic inability?" Bessie asked.

"Because," I answered, "the dumbhead didn't want Chrissie to know what a nut her mother was."

Bessie looked at me, incredulous. "And she didn't know?"

"Of course she knew. She didn't say anything because she didn't want to upset Jim."

Bessie threw up her hands. "Families! How do you know all this, anyway?"

"After her mother died, Jim asked me to talk with Chrissie and give her my version of grief counseling. During our talk, she told me all.

"She's really a remarkable kid. Extremely bright. Beautiful. Serious about her studies. If she weren't such a sweetheart, it would be easy to hate her. As it is, she's lovable and I love her."

Our hamburgers arrived and engaged our attention.

The Forensic Lab occupies a one-story building a little bit north of LIT and just past the DRA complex. I parked and entered. A reception desk was close by. I gave the guard my identification card and he picked up the phone. A few minutes later a portly, white haired, goateed gentleman wearing a white jacket arrived at the desk. He was either Colonel Sanders or someone in a lab coat. He stuck out his hand. "I'm Paul Richards. You're Bea?" Not Sanders then; his accent was pure middle America.

I acknowledged my identity and shook his hand.

I followed Paul through a set of double doors and into his territory. "Let me give you a quick Cook's tour before we settle down to talk." We were walking down a wide, very clean corridor. Private offices lined one side of the corridor, a few other, larger rooms were on the other side. Paul stopped by one of the larger rooms and collected two pair of protective glasses. We put them on before we walked into the vestibule of the lab. Paul explained that there was a larger room for evidence examination, but the room we were about to enter was strictly for PCR set-up. Some less prosperous labs combined those two room, but Paul's was among the elite facilities.

"Whoa," Paul said, "this is as far as you aliens can go. We handle DNA evidence in this room. Contamination can be a problem, so we restrict entry to those who need to enter.

"We all have security cards. New cards with a new wrinkle were issued a couple of months ago. Now, every access is recorded by date, time, and team number, so we can identify the team to which someone who enters belongs and when the access took place. The Departmental secretary and I each have our own card. I don't think the staff realizes how much information is stored on these little cards.

"One of those security cards is needed to get into this room, which is the PCR set up room. Incidentally, that stands for polymerase chain reaction. It's a technology that amplifies a piece of DNA, to get thousands, even millions, of copies, of a given DNA fragment. So once we extract the DNA from evidence, we bring it here to prepare it for amplification. I'll talk to you a little later about the problem we're having with the astounding disappearing reagents, which are kept in this room. Meanwhile, let's take a look at the lab where the amplification takes place."

We passed a bulge in the corridor where the Departmental secretary's desk was located. It was currently uninhabited. Paul said, "Bridget is faxing some stuff for me. You'll meet her later."

We walked into the vestibule of another large room. This time Paul fetched a lab coat for me and retrieved latex gloves for both of us from a small cabinet. Once we were appropriately garbed, Paul led me into the lab. "It's okay for you aliens to enter here. There's no danger of contamination in the post PCR room, where the process is finished off."

He patted an instrument about the size of a small suitcase. I asked "What's that humming noise?"

Paul laughed. "Cutting edge technology. It's a fan that runs constantly. Those occasional clicks that you hear are the machine doing its work. The machine is called a 'thermal cycle' where DNA-in-waiting is subjected to a series of heating and cooling cycles."

I watched the temperature rise to 96 Celsius (240.8 Fahrenheit) on the instrument's panel and hold for a minute before the machine clicked and the temperature started falling.

Paul explained, "It takes the alternating heating and cooling to open up the DNA strands and then to let the polymerase enzyme copy a new strand. With each cycle we double the amount of DNA in the reaction."

By this time, my eyes were glazing over, my ears were threatening to shut down, and I could feel a nap coming on. Standing up. Please God don't let me snore.

"Am I boring you?" Paul asked.

I jerked awake. "No, no. Not at all. This is absolutely riveting."

Satisfied, Paul happily led me to a bench that held several plastic trays. "For tests that use PCR, we take the amplified DNA and use these thin nylon membranes to capture the amplified fragments.

"On these membranes are specific regions that will match the exact sequence of the amplified DNA. Then we add a chemical that undergoes a chemical reaction to produce a blue dot on the membrane wherever the DNA has attached."

Paul showed me a membrane. "For example – at this marker, called 'DQ-alpha' this person has the '2' dot showing and the '3' dot showing. We would say that this person is a '2,3' at this marker. Here's another example. You can see that the '1' dot is highlighted along with the '3' dot. However – now this is fascinating – we can break down the '1' dot into sub-categories."

I looked to the right across the membrane and noticed other dots were highlighted.

"Specifically", Paul said, "this person has the 1.1, sub-type to go with the 3. So what do you think that would make him?"

Thank you, Lord, for waking me up before I slept through the exam. "A 1.1,3." Triumphantly.

"You're hired," Paul announced.

As we started toward the door, Paul noted that PCR testing isn't the only type of DNA testing. Mitochondrial testing, which traces the subject's maternal history, for instance, can be useful when you want to know the ethnic group of the subject. There were gel boxes in the lab for other types of test. Those tests required computer imaging.

For one frantic moment I thought he was going to go through every test known to humankind. Would the lecture encompass alchemy? I might stay awake for that. But no. The schoolroom session was over.

We left the room, shed our gear, and walked toward Paul's office. "That computer we're using for the non-PCR testing was the cat's pajamas when we got it. But now." He shrugged. "IBM is about to come out with the new Pentium3 desktops which are incredibly faster. But will we get some? Not in my lifetime. You ever heard of Jack Brooks?"

"I have, indeed." Congressman Brooks chairs the Government Operations committee which, in the name of accountability, has prevented all government agencies from acquiring an effective infrastructure.

Paul continued. "The Federal government used to be able to get the state-of-the-art technology that let us do our job better and quicker. But now the paperwork and approvals and whatall take so much time that any technology we order is obsolete before it gets here. Lord knows how much money they waste on the pencil pushers that move a request through the system."

Paul motioned me into his office. It wasn't as large or as comfortable as Pie's office. The Department of Justice's pecking order must be different from DoTI's. But it was a sizable room, albeit plainly furnished. In deference to his position as Director, the standard metal desk had given way to the standard wooden desk, on which sat the standard pictures of his wife and family. Were those pictures standard issue or were the ones on his desk really of his family? Keep your mind on business, Bea.

We seated ourselves at a small round table which, I surmised, was used for team meetings. "Before we get to the reason why we asked for your help, let me explain this lab. For years, we were a run-of-the-mill forensic lab, capable of performing routine tests. For anything beyond that, there were a few private labs, plus the FBI which had every conceivable capability. Then a few years ago we joined that little group.

"What happened to us was Congress, specifically the Judiciary Committee. The Committee decided that with all the new advances in forensic technology, the FBI would get overwhelmed with requests from the states and municipalities for assistance in criminal investigations. Another facility was needed to help with the non-criminal stuff. They picked my lab and threw money at us. I'm not sure exactly why that happened. My guess is that the FBI and my lab are overseen by different sub-committees of the Judiciary Committee and our guys wanted in on the action.

"A lot of our staff has been here since before the upgrade. The rest, including Cody Kletsch – he's the Team 3 supervisor – we stole from state or university labs.

"So here's the crux of the problem," Paul said. He handed me a small cardboard box.

"This is an example of the DQ-alpha kit that we use for the PCR test. Inside this unassuming little box there usually are a couple of critical reagents. One contains the PCR primers that get added to the DNA in the PCR room. The other would be the critical DNA polymerase that does the actual copying during the thermal cycler phase. It isn't in the box now, because that enzyme has to be stored in the freezer until use. Now, that enzyme is critical to the success of the assay since most enzymes go inactive after being heated to such high temperatures. But *this* enzyme comes from a bacteria that has evolved to live in a geothermal vent. It might as well be called 'Fort Knox' because its price rivals that of gold. It's expensive as hell, if you'll pardon my French, and someone on Team 3 is making off with armloads of it and is selling it to someone or someones in the biotech community who don't mind buying a little something under the table at a discount.

"I really appreciate you doing this, Bea. Those reagents are not walking out the door, they're galloping. How do you want to proceed?"

"I take it that you've narrowed the suspects down to Team 3, based on the information from the security cards."

Paul nodded.

" I'd like to meet each member of the team today. We can set up appointments to meet again on Monday. I want to give them at least a day to get used to the idea and Friday's not a good day for serious discussion, anyway. Everyone always wants to clear up the week's work and get out early."

Paul pursed his lips, nodded agreement, tugged at his goatee, and said, "Sounds good. There are four team members: a supervisor, an analyst, and two technicians. The team would ordinarily have two analysts but we got caught in a budget crunch so we're one down.

"Let's start with Cody Kletsch. He's the team's supervisor. Nice, affable guy. He's a transplanted Californian. I don't know what brought him East. He's capable, doesn't pull rank. If the lab is backed up he takes part of the load himself. We're lucky to have him. Come on."

Paul lumbered off with me in his wake.

Cody Kletsch was garbed in khakis and an open-necked plaid shirt. He was a middle-sized guy in his mid-fifties. His graying hair was cropped close, his gray eyes had inviting crinkles at the corners, and he appeared to be in fighting trim. He regarded me. "Management audit, huh? Who decreed the audit?"

I grinned at him. "Order came from above. It's happening all over the Department. I got you because my normal place of business is just up the road at LIT. I don't have to go far to get here." How's that for a cover story?

"Well, what can't be cured must be endured, as the saying goes. So what do we have to do to endure you?"

"Schedule some appointments for Monday, answer some questions, talk about whatever you want to talk about, and if you have some cookies, share them."

Cody guffawed. "Lady, we don't have a crust of bread. For food, we share the DRA cafeteria and are lucky to get that."

"Rats. Will you set up half-hour appointments for me with your staff or should I set them up individually myself?"

"I'll set them up. How long will they take and when do you want to start?"

"Let's start at 10:30 Monday and take half an hour each. If any of the interviews look like they're running over, I'll come back to finish."

"Sold. The schedule will be with the guard at the desk when you arrive."

"Paul said you were from California. What brought you here?"

"I had a post-doc at the Armed Forces Institute of Pathology and then I lab-hopped to a few different places around the country. I was in North Carolina when Paul's lab got the star treatment and he recruited me. I couldn't ask for a better place to be. We've got every toy a forensic scientist could dream of."

"Do you miss California?"

Cody chuckled. "Yeah, when it snows here. I was born in the Bay area, in Alameda. It was a great place to grow up."

"You must have been there when Pearl Harbor was bombed."

"Yeah. I was about seven. There weren't many Japanese there at the time, but those that were got moved off to the internment camps. They were there one day and the next, poof, they were gone.

"It was for their own good, you know. There were a lot of bad feelings toward them and the government was afraid they'd get hurt if they weren't protected. Still, it was a bad business. A real bad business. But time has passed and no lasting harm was done."

"So you're here to stay?"

"You betcha. I've got a nice hunk of land in Alexandria, a little house and a great big dog who makes living worthwhile."

"Big like a Newfoundland?"

Cody laughed. "Not that big. It's a silver Lab. Bodonkey's a little over a year old and rambunctious as hell. I want to bring him to work, but Paul won't let me. I don't know why. Dixie Lee Ray brought her dog to the office every day that she was Governor of Washington State and nothing bad happened."

"Well," I said, "maybe Paul doesn't think that a lab full of bones is quite the place for a big, rambunctious mutt."

"Hmmm, I never thought of that. Maybe he has a point." Cody looked at his watch and I stood up.

"Thanks for your time, Cody. I'd better go meet the rest of your staff. I'll talk with you again Monday and maybe I'll be able to stick to topic."

"Don't try too hard. It's more fun talking about old times."

Elliott Giles, one of the two technicians, was next. He was a softish, pasty looking man. He looked like he avoided both the sun and exertion whenever possible. His comb-over was an unconvincing black – unconvincing partly because some of the dye adhered to his scalp. Whereas Cody Kletsch was amiable, loose, and quick to laugh, Giles was buttoned up, tight lipped, and mindful of his rightful place in the world. "In case you are interested in my credentials," he said as soon as I sat down, "I received my Master's in Forensic Science from the University of Alabama-Birmingham in 1989."

He looked older than someone with a 1989 Master's degree. He either started college late or took time off between Bachelor's and Master's.

I said, "The school has an excellent reputation. Do you live close to the Forensics Lab?"

"Not at all," he said. "I live in Winchester, Virginia." His lush Virginia accent made him sound like Sonny Jurgenson. "Do *you* live nearby?"

I smiled. "Not at all. I live in Alexandria, Virginia."

Giles seemed marginally warmer. "A fine old town." He was one of those people who smile with lips closed. He proceeded to do just that. "Do you know how long ago it was founded?"

"Yes. 1749."

"Well, now," said Giles, getting warmer by the minute, "that is indeed gratifying. You know, my lineage goes back even farther.

The father of my illustrious ancestor, James Madison, was an early tobacco farmer in Orange, Virginia. Can you imagine that area? Mr. Madison, Mr. Jefferson, and Mr. Monroe all living cheek-by-jowl."

"That was indeed some neighborhood! Is that why you choose to live in Virginia?"

"Well, yes. Of course. Just can't abide these Maryland Yankees." He chuckled, but I had the feeling that he really wasn't joking.

I told him that I'd be back Monday to get his valuable advice on the management and organization of the Lab. We parted on excellent terms.

On my way to see Yvonne Danielson, the other technician, I had to pass the desk of the Departmental secretary. It was now occupied by said secretary, Bridget Perry. It was an interesting tableau. Perry, herself, was a big breasted, creamy skinned, full lipped, utterly magnificent woman in her thirties. Standing behind her was an attractive Japanese-American woman in her mid-fifties. I took her to be the team's analyst, Jasmine Nishiyama. In front of the the desk was a man, also in his fifties, wearing a scruffy toupee and trying to get a peek down Perry's decolletage. Rounding out the scene was a twenty-ish kid who looked like a younger version of the peeker. I drew up short.

The Asian woman came around the desk and extended her hand. She was indeed Jasmine Nishiyama. "Everyone calls me Jazz. You're Dr. Goode?'

I admitted it.

She nodded to the older man. This is Congressman Jimboy

Davies and that," she gestured at the kid, "is Jimboy Jr."

The Congressman did not abandon his quest for a peek. Junior cast a hopeful glance toward my bosom. Alas. I was wearing a crew neck tee under a blazer. Tough luck, sonny.

Jazz was stifling a laugh. "Who have you seen so far?"

"Paul, Cody, and Elliot. I'm on my way to see Yvonne Danielson."

Jazz nodded. "I'll be free as soon as the Congressman concludes his business."

The Congressman shot her a poisonous look. Now what was all that about?

Danielson was a nondescript woman. Unremarkable build. Light brown hair tightly curled. Pale eyes. Spoke through the almost-clenched teeth indicative of Seven Sisters lockjaw. Mount Holyoke as it turned out. She had been at the Forensic Lab for about two years, after getting her Masters at George Washington University. She asked if I had spoken to Cody yet.

"I have. Seems like a nice guy."

Danielson looked at me. "He'd be a lot nicer if he spoke less."

I waited for her to go on but all that ensued was silence.

"What do you mean by that, Yvonne?"

"Nothing. I shouldn't have said anything. Forget it."

This conversation was clearly going nowhere, so I said good-bye and walked to Jazz's office. The corridors here are strangely quiet. This is unlike LIT, where office doors are usually open and scientists confer on the fly.

Jazz appeared shortly. "Good grief," she said. "I think those sleazes thought they could wait me out."

"I'm clueless. Please tell all."

Jazz grinned. "Jimboy Davies, esteemed member of our Authorization Committee, is a lech. I think he comes from a Congressional district populated by leches. About ten years ago he was accused of having sex with a fourteen-year-old girl. The jury was out all of ten minutes before they acquitted him. Jimboy junior is a chip off the old block.

"About six months ago, the Committee came to pay us an inspection visit and Jimboy took one look at Bridget and his eyeballs bulged and his tongue hung out. He started coming around to 'follow up' the inspection and, of course, stopped to say "howdy ma'am" to Bridget. After the third inspection, Bridget complained to Paul – the sleaze was having trouble keeping his hands to himself. "So now, when he comes, unannounced, to call, Paul gets warned by the fella at the desk and one of us stands guard at Bridget's desk until he leaves. Today was my turn for Jimboy duty.

"How did your interviews go?"

"This was just get-acquainted day. The real interviews start Monday. How long have you been here?"

"About 10 years. I spent most of my life in California."

"Where there?"

"I was born in Alameda."

"Really! Did you know Cody?"

"I knew Cody. Cody didn't know me."

"Would you care to elaborate?"

Jazz waited a few beats then said, "Why not? Do you know

anything about the Japanese incarceration during the War?"

"Not much. Just that it was wildly unfair and it took over 40 years before the government acknowledged that we had done anything wrong."

"That's more than most people know. There weren't that many of us Nisei in Alameda – less than one percent of the population – when Pearl Harbor happened. But those few of us were reasonably prosperous. Well, the evacuation order came. We had to pack up our stuff and leave for a camp. We could only take one or two bags, I don't remember whether it was one or two. Certainly no more than two. Everything else had to be left behind.

"Since we only had a few days to get out, all of our property was up for quick sale. A few of us were lucky enough to have White friends who kept their property for them until the war ended. We weren't lucky. My grandfather owned a general store. You know, the kind that carries dry goods, and some fruit and vegetables, a little bit of meat, sundries, and a big gumball machine. I was about four years old at the time and didn't understand what was going on. Why was everyone crying? Who was that White guy arguing with Grampa?

"Well, that White guy was offering my grandfather about two cents on the dollar for the whole shebang, including the building. We had no choice. Grampa went from prosperous to wiped-out in an eye blink. While all that was going on, I was sitting on the floor and a little White kid, a few years older than me, was putting pennies in the gumball machine, filling his fist with gumballs and peppering me with the damn things. Each time he hit me he hollered 'Take that, Slant!'.

The guy who cheated Grampa was Cody Kletsch's grandfather. The kid was Cody.

"Fifty years have gone by, Bea, but some things you don't forget. Some things still hurt."

"Does Cody know who you are?"

"No. Are you going to tell him?

"No." With that, I left.

I checked in with Pie when I got back to LIT. "Pie, during World War II did you have a hard time or did people recognize the difference between Chinese and Japanese?"

"Why are you asking?"

I repeated Jazz Nishiyama's story.

Pie winced. "It was different on the East Coast. Particularly in New York. And it helped that I lived in a Jewish community. No one was willing to give up their egg foo yong." He laughed. "You could always tell a Jewish neighborhood by the large number of Chinese restaurants."

"You still can."

CHAPTER 3

May 21 - 23, 1993

Our house sits on one of the last cobblestone streets left in Alexandria. It's a narrow, three-story, neo-Federalist house just one large room wide, with a staircase to the left of the door as you walk in. A little over a year ago we did some remodeling. Moved the kitchen, which had been on the second floor to the first. Moved the displaced living room to the second floor. And left the bedroom intact on the third floor.

A partition separates a kitchen large enough to hold a breakfast table, from the dining room, that seats a comfortable eight. The kitchen leads out to a little graveled patio studded with potted plants. We aren't adept gardeners. The potted plants are frequently changed as one plant dies and a replacement is selected. Shopping for new plants is more fun than maintaining old ones.

The only way to get to the basement is through the patio, and the only way to get to the patio is through the house. That's because the houses on our block sit right against one another. Our patio is separated from the patio on the left by a high cedar-board fence. The current owner installed it when he moved in a couple of years ago. We're separated from the patio on the right by a much friendlier short picket fence. We back onto a similar house, separated from us by a split-rail fence, which our backside neighbor installed. In the words of Ralph Waldo Emerson, "A foolish consistency is the hobgoblin of little fence builders." (At least he said something like that). Unlike our block, the houses there have narrow walkways separating them. The residents can reach their patios without going through the house.

The basement is where we store all of the stuff that we don't need now, but will someday be useful. By which time we'll have forgotten where we put it.

We know our neighbors, but it's not a cozy neighborhood the way some suburban neighborhoods are. For that kind of koffee klatsching friendly, you need kids. And kids don't fit in these little houses. But we like one another well enough, help one another out in a pinch, and generally get along pretty well, except for the guy on the other side of the cedar-board fence who is known to all as "the sonuvabitch who won't shovel his walk".

We stuck our heads out the back door to confirm that this was going to be a glorious, top-down day. Happily, we opened the front door and discovered that the Mustang was blocked by a double-parked moving truck, inscribed 'Two Guys Who Haul Stuff'. The two guys were removing furniture from the house of the aforementioned sonuvabitch.

Alex trotted down the stairs and said, "Could you move your truck so that we can get out?"

One of the guys, the one who was only slightly smaller than his truck, shook his head. He jerked his thumb at the sonuvabitch's house. "He told us to park here so he could get his car out."

"Well, I'm telling you to park *there* so that we can get *our* car out."

The mover snickered. "You ain't payin' us. He is." He

turned back to his truck. Just then an Alexandria police car began to inch its way around the truck on the way to God knows where. Alex waved his arms and the cop stopped.

"You got a problem?"

Alex explained the situation while the movers extracted a sofa from the house.

The cop looked at the big guy. "Move the truck."

"We'll be done right away." The two movers muscled the sofa into the back of the van.

The cop peered into the truck, which was nearly empty. "You moving the whole house?"

"Yeah."

"You'll be here all day. Move the truck."

"No way!"

The cop took out his pad and prepared to write a ticket.

"Hey, I ain't Mayflower. I can't afford no tickets."

"Then move the truck or we'll move it for you. Think you can afford to retrieve it from the tow yard?"

"Goddammit, we're just tryin' to earn a honest living."

"Move the truck or I'll have it towed with the furniture in it."

At that moment, the sonuvabitch, dressed in pajamas, robe, and slippers came down the stairs, smiling at the cop. "What's the problem, officer?"

The cop explained. The sonuvabitch held out his hand to shake. "I'm sure we can settle this amicably."

The cop shook and opened his right hand to discover a greenback in it.

"Are you trying to bribe me, you moron?"

"Who you calling a moron?"

"The moron who's trying to bribe me in front of two witnesses."

Meanwhile, most of the neighborhood was enjoying the show. The guy who lived on the other side of us entered the conversation, "More than two. Most of us would be happy to testify. He's the sonuvabitch who won't shovel his walk."

The cop turned to the mover. "Move the effing truck or I'll take you with us when I haul your boss in."

The truck was moved. The sonuvabitch was ushered – pajamas, robe, slippers, and all – into the squad car. God was in heaven, all was right with the world.

Alex and I were still chortling over the exchange when we reached the turnoff from the beltway to the LIT road. That intersection used to be graced by an Alligator Wrestling Emporium. It is now an empty shed. Last Memorial Day, while we were attending the town of Bella Villa's celebration, the owner of the Emporium let a boa constrictor loose on the green.[3] Alex, my hero, brained the snake with the mallet from the strength-o-meter. The snake's owner was outraged. I don't know if that incident had anything to do with the demise of the Emporium, but the business is gone, leaving only the shed as a reminder of its glory days.

Alex negotiated the turn and said, *"The first mathematician was Adam."*

"How do you get that? Mathematics wasn't developed until

[3] See *A Fine Climate for Murder*

we had real civilizations. Like Mayans, Greeks, Egyptians, all those."

"This is fiction," Alex explained. "Besides, who said it was *that* Adam?"

"Okay. Let's establish that right now. *Who spied apples on those trees that had 'em.*"

Alex thought for a minute, then smiled evilly at me. "I gotcha now. *He took one from from Eve and said I believe,*"

I returned the evil grin. "In your dreams. *We should multiply fruitfully, Madam*"

Alex groaned. "That's terrible!"

"Since when are you the jury?"

"They'll support me in this, you'll see."

Alex pulled into our parking space, debarked, and addressed the multitude.

> *"The first mathematician was Adam,*
> *Who spied apples on those trees that had 'em,*
> *He took one from Eve,*
> *And said, "I believe*
> *We should multiply fruitfully, Madam."*

The multitude caucused. Time passed. Lenore walked by, shaking her head. Finally, the verdict was announced. Cheers and huzzahs.

Alex turned to me. "I hope you noticed that there were many abstentions."

I shrugged. "Creationists, no doubt."

Don walked with me down the admin corridor.

"How's the remodeling going, Don?"

"You wouldn't believe what happened."

"Try me."

"Connie and I went out for a burger after work and when we got home, a fire engine was parked in front of the house and firemen were running all over looking for a fire. A couple of them broke through the temporary door that the contractor put up. They went tearing through the house looking for smoke. Finally they decided that where there was no smoke there was no fire, and they went looking to see what set off the alarm. They figured out that the contractor hadn't covered up the fire alarm unit and it got filled with debris. That set off the alarm that rings in the firehouse and they sent a truck to put out the fire. We're gonna get hit with a big bill for causing a false alarm."

"Can you collect from the contractor?"

"I guess so. We'll probably deduct it from his final payment."

I laughed. "I can hardly wait for the next installment of the Remodeling Follies."

I hate retirement parties. These are gatherings to say good-bye to someone who half the people attending either don't know or can't stand. I've solved my refusal to attend by letting it be known that I will only attend those parties being held for someone I'm glad to see leave. That lets me off the hook in the kindest possible way. Thus, the call from Chrissie – daughter of Jim Daly and intern of Molly Cameron – came as a surprise.

Chrissie is a tall, leggy, blonde who has no idea how

devastatingly gorgeous she is. Or if she does have some idea, she doesn't let on.

"Dr. Goode, Ken Austin is retiring and he would really like you to be at the party on Monday evening. He really, really admires you. Would you please come?"

Now what on earth brought that on? Austin barely knows me and vice versa. "Chrissie, did Molly Cameron put you up to this? Is she getting even for having to be nice to the Constituent?"

Silence.

"Chrissie, what did she promise you for making this call?"

"Gee, Dr. Goode, are you mad at me?"

"No, Chrissie, of course not. Unless you won't tell me what she promised."

Chrissie had no compunction about betraying her boss. "Well, Dr. Hodler wants to quit and come back part-time because she's going to have a baby. When she quits it will free up a position and Dr. Cameron said she'd advertise it as two half-time positions and give me and Dr. Hodler the two half-times. But first I had to talk you into coming to the party."

I burst out laughing. "Okay, far be it from me to derail your promising career. But you tell Molly that I'm going to drink myself pie-eyed through the speeches and throw up at the end of the evening.

"I'll tell her, but I don't believe you'll do it. She won't believe it, either."

"Skeptics that you are, you might not believe it but you'll never be sure until the evening's over. Serve you both right."

I hung up and called Ralph Manley, Chrissie's mentor. I

explained the situation to him. "Ralph, can you smuggle a gallon jug into the banquet room?"

He was laughing. "Sure, what do you want it for?"

"I want to hide it under the table. Then I'll order a drink every time Molly looks my way and pour it into the jug when she's not looking."

Ralph was laughing harder. Once he composed himself, he said. "I'd better bring a wide-mouthed jug. We don't want booze spilled all over the floor." He was laughing again when we hung up.

The government clunker was waiting to bear me to the Forensic Lab. I got in, turned the key, and got an anemic whine. I discussed this with the clunker, speaking softly, and issuing complimentary phrases. More whines. I finally changed tactics and yelled. "*Start* you miserable bag of bolts or I'll tear your hubcaps off one by one!"

The car started and, together, we motored to our destination. There's more than one way to skin a car.

The Lab was humming with excitement when I arrived. Human bones had been found Thursday, washed up on Bloodsworth Island. The bones were identified as the left arm bones of an adult male. Under the bones was a gold watch inscribed "to Adam with timeless love." The package arrived at the Lab on Friday. The watch was the single clue to the identity of the bones. But several years ago, while sailing solo in the Chesapeake Bay, Adam Brattice's boat capsized. The boat was found but Brattice was not. Since the man was a billionaire, this caused more than the usual stir. To Team 3's delight, it received the assignment.

On receipt of the bones, Paul immediately attempted to contact Brattice's wife. The housekeeper answered the phone. She told Paul that Mrs. Brattice, young Adam junior, and Brattice's brother, Howard, had just left for a ski weekend in Colorado. But Brattice's sister lived nearby.

Paul contacted the sister. She confirmed that her brother had a watch fitting that description. Paul then asked if she knew if there might possibly be a preserved sample of Adam's blood. The woman laughed. There was a contract, related to their business, that was stored in her safe. When signing it, Adam had suffered a small paper cut which bled a bit onto the paper.

"The reason I remember the cut," she said, "is that the fuss Adam made over it would have been an appropriate response to the swipe of a cutlass."

Paul offered to send someone to collect the paper, but she was curious about the activities of a forensic lab and would deliver it herself. While she was at it, she would verify that the watch was her brother's.

Bloodsworth is a small Chesapeake Bay island in Dorchester County, Maryland about thirty miles northwest of Salisbury University. The Navy uses it as a practice range, firing or dropping live munitions that contain explosives. Some of the explosives don't explode, so there is unexploded ordnance scattered around the island. It is not a prudent place to go camping, although the resident birds and migrating water fowl find it congenial. For some arcane reason, waterfowl nest there. Of particular interest to wildfowl photographers are the heron rookeries. Despite the disturbance caused by the Navy's pummeling of the island, the birds remain and the photographers want to take their picture. Usually the photos are taken from a boat. But once in a while, a photographer would like a land-based angle. Last Wednesday, a couple of intrepid photographers received permission to land on the island and to very carefully get within photo-shoot range. This they did on Thursday, which was when they discovered the bone fragments. The bone marrow was long gone, but the fragments, particularly one large fragment, looked a lot like remnants of a human body.

The photographers completed their photo shoot. Then they thought it might be a good idea to bring the fragments to the police station in case it turned out to be a missing person. The cops, after dithering a day, decided to bring the bones to the Forensic Lab. And thus was Adam Brattice identified. His wife and sister were so informed and then things got interesting.

I learned this while sitting in Paul's office. He was clearly enjoying the legal muddle.

"It's like this, Bea. In Maryland, a missing person isn't considered legally dead until seven years have passed. So until we confirmed that the bones were his, he was still legally alive. Would be, for a few more months. His son was, of course, in the care of his mother who, therefore, had access to the Brattice billions.

"Well, Brattice's will specifies that with the exception of a few small bequests, his sole heir is his son. Doesn't name the kid, just says 'my son'. Now, the law is pretty explicit. When a will says "son", it means biological son unless he's specified by name – which isn't the case here – or the putative father adopted the kid which also isn't the case since why would he adopt a kid he believed was his own? Follow?"

"I'm with you so far, Paul."

He stroked his goatee and chuckled. "Well, the will also specifies that if his son predeceases him, the bulk of his billions goes to his sister, who is a twenty percent partner in the business that made all that money. His wife would only get half a million.

"There's a lot of money at stake, a fact that did not escape Ms. Eunice Hunter, Brattice's sister. She and her husband immediately claimed that Adam was not young Brat's father and she should get the inheritance. That's not quite clear, but there's at least a fifty-fifty chance that the Hunters would inherit if it's not his son. Brattice had told her that he had a very low sperm count and was surprised and delighted that he fathered the kid. Eunice had held her tongue, but she knew that Adam's wife had been playing around and she now questions the parenthood. She wants the kid's DNA analyzed."

"It sounds like she and Adam were close."

Paul settled back in his chair in order to get comfortable for a good gossip. "They were. She has that twenty percent interest in his business ventures. And you don't have to be good at math to understand that twenty percent of billions is a lot. The Hunters aren't hurting for money.

"I met them when Eunice and her husband came in to verify the watch and deliver Adam's preserved blood sample. Because there's so much at stake we also took Eunice's blood sample. We'll do a mitochondrial DNA test. That'll tell us if she and Adam are in the same family. If it comes to a lawsuit, we'd better have all the evidence it's possible to get.

"The Hunters stayed for a cup of coffee and a chat. Seem like nice people. They don't have much use for the third sibling, though. That's Howard Brattice who has made his own money, but not in a league with Adam. Howard, by the way, is not a natural sibling. Mrs. Hunter said that he was adopted by their parents when, after trying for several years to have a kid, they gave up and adopted one. And, as so often happens, as soon as the kid was adopted, they produced a couple of their own. Howard's DNA wouldn't have done us any good."

I nodded. "I wonder why that happens. A couple I knew adopted and then went on to produce four more kids on their own. When they left the area they were trying for a fifth."

Paul drew back. "They wanted six kids? Seems to me that's four too many."

I changed the subject back. "If the Hunters are wealthy in their own right, why are they trying to get more?" I asked.

"Understandable spite. The person Adam's wife has been canoodling with is Howard Brattice, their brother. Howard told Eunice about it, in order to get himself a good gloat. She never said anything in deference to Adam's feelings. My understanding is that if she gets the money she'll set up a trust fund for young Brat with herself as executor. Keeps the money out of the hands of Mrs. Brattice and Howard."

"What about the kid? What kind of person is he?"

"The Hunters are fond of him. They say that he was devoted to Adam and is close to his mother. He's not overly fond of Howard."

"When," I asked Paul, "was the last time you had this much

fun in the Lab?"

"Would you believe 'never'?"

Through a mixture of cajolery and threats, I convinced the clunker to get me back to LIT. Gasping, it eventually pulled into its parking place.

I waved at Lenore, knocked, and entered Pie's office. For once he wasn't either on the phone or engaged in budget struggles with Don.

"Hey, Pie. Did you unload the Very *Very* Important Constituent?"

"Handed him off to Molly who was being overwhelmingly gracious. I thought she was overdoing it, but the Constituent seemed pleased. I wonder why she went overboard like that."

I laughed. "She thinks she's getting even with me." I explained the nefarious plan.

"You realize, do you not, that you are about to bring a load of *tsores* down on your *kup*? Molly will be out for revenge."

"I know. But it'll be worth it."

Pie was still laughing when Don walked in. I went through the whole routine again.

Don said, "You know this will mean war."

"I shall prepare for battle."

"I'd invite myself to the retirement party," he said, "but Molly'd smell a rat. Take good notes.

"So how's it going at the Forensic Lab? You making any progress?"

"No progress on catching the reagent thief, but it sure is

getting interesting." I told the tale with appropriate dramatic emphasis.

Don remarked, "So they believe that if it's not his kid, then his sister gets the bucks."

I nodded. "Not certain, but a fightin' chance."

"Then," said Dr. P.I. Lee, "if it's not his kid, Momma gets *bubkes*?"

"Well, if you think half a million is *bubkes*," I answered, "then Momma gets *bubkes*."

Don passed considered judgement. "It'd serve serve her right."

Alex and I had dinner at The Rabbit Hole and arrived at the cabin sated and happy. Our landlords, Daryl and Claudia Coker, wandered by as we were sitting on the front step enjoying the evening. Claudia said, "Daryl Jr. and Sandy are coming over tomorrow for dinner. Can you join us?"

"With pleasure," Alex said. "What can we bring?"

Daryl remarked, "You don't have anything in that cabin *to* bring."

"On the contrary," Alex responded, "we have lots of beer."

And so it was decided.

We spent most of Saturday being very busy doing nothing much. We dug around in our little herb garden. We cuddled the animals. We took a walk in the nearby woods. May is a great time for mooching around in the woods. The spring beauties dot the landscape. The trilliums and the jack in the pulpits haven't faded yet. Some of the bluebells are still hanging on. The bloodroots are putting on a show. May apple blooms are peeking from under the leaves. If you should chance to look up, dogwoods and mountain laurels are there to entertain you. And permeating the entire scene is the indefinable scent of woods in the spring. Eventually, we abandoned the trees in favor of sitting on our front step and having a glass of wine.

Around six, we heard Junior's truck pull up and we lugged a case of beer over to greet them. Both of the young Cokers teach at Oxford College – Junior in the math department, Sandy in biology. Junior looked a lot like his dad. He was about five foot nine, with dimpled cheeks and an engaging smile. He had his dad's straw colored hair but was missing his dad's mustache. Sandy was about my five foot four height with glossy brown hair and a benevolent look about her.

As always at gatherings at the elder Cokers, Alex and Junior retreated into their own world of technology and Claudia shooed Sandy and me out of the kitchen. We two wandered outdoors. The normally ebullient Sandy was looking morose.

"Is something wrong?" I asked.

"Damn right," she said. "I need an animal to cuddle."

We walked over to the paddock where Louise the Llama came to pay her respects. She stuck her head over the fence and Sandy nuzzled her.

"Are you going to share your troubles only with Louise or can I help?"

Sandy started to cry. "Oh, Bea, why are people so horrible?" She dug in her pocket and extracted a Kleenex.

"What happened?"

"One of our neighbors, Olga Bielev, had a really sweet dog, a little mutt named Sugar. Sugar was a service dog, trained to warn Olga when her blood sugar was getting low. She didn't have to be with Olga every minute of the day, so Sugar could visit some of the other neighbors for short spells. She particularly loved the Janssauds who kept treats for her and sometimes took her for little walks. Olga and the Janssauds were really close – Olga had helped them out of a couple of financial jams. And they agreed that if Olga died before Sugar, the Janssauds would make a home for the little mutt. Well, Olga died last week when the college was on spring break and Daryl and I were on a short cruise.

"When we came back the Jannsauds told us about Olga dying and that they decided to get a dog of their own, so they had Sugar put down." Sandy started to cry again.

"That gentle little dog thought she was part of their family and those miserable weasels had her put down. Didn't matter what they promised Olga. After all, she was dead and couldn't pony up money when they needed it!"

"Did you ask why they didn't wait for you to come home?"

Sandy sniffed. "Yeah. We'd have taken Sugar like a shot. But the bastards said that if Sugar stayed in the neighborhood she would try to come visit them and would disrupt the training of their new pet. It's an Alsatian and I hope he bites them!"

She laid her head next to Louise, who nuzzled her sympathetically.

Eventually, Sandy straightened up and gave Louise a farewell pat.

We walked back to the house where we found Big Daryl

about to emerge for the purpose of calling us. The Cokers have a typical farm house. As you walk through the door you are immediately in the kitchen. To the left is a large refrigerator; to the right a major counter that hugs one wall, pauses for the six-burner, double-oven stove, and joins the connecting wall that contains a farm sink below a big window. A farm sink, by the way, is a huge, deep, low, white enamel affair that will take a banquet load of dirty dishes. A very large dish washer completes the tour of the perimeter. In the middle of the kitchen is a rough-hewn table that could probably seat ten without effort.

Big Daryl, Junior, and Alex had set the table. Claudia was bringing out the food. It was a typical Maryland farm dinner – deviled eggs to start, split pea and ham soup, crab cake salad, prime rib with horseradish mashed potatoes, and roasted parsnips on the side. Plus a Dover cake to finish it off. Great meal.

Sandy even forgot about Sugar long enough to enjoy herself.

A light drizzle kept us in on Sunday. It was a particularly annoying drizzle – not enough water to prevent a serious drought, but enough to prevent us from taking a pleasant hike. Ah well, since we were due at Pie's and Bessie's for dinner, Alex could use the indoor time to make our contribution to Bessie's feast – his world-famous almond meringue cookies, a remarkable feat as performed in the cabin's tiny kitchen. Well, maybe they aren't world-famous. LIT-famous, anyway. We'd find something else to do with the rest of the time indoors.

Pie and Bessie live in a remodeled farmhouse not too far from LIT and just up the road from our cabin. Bessie is a little dumpling of a woman who loves to cook, particularly for guests. Her kitchen was built as if for a three star chef. Which she could well have been if she weren't an illustrious archeologist, as eminent in her field as Pie is in his. She cooks between digs.

Bessie's dinner was on the other end of the continent from Claudia's. She had made a peppered roast duckling in one of her neo-Etruscan pots. She served it with cooked fennel, red cabbage, and little roast potatoes. As we gnawed on the bones the subject of Jeanne's and Jim's wedding arose. "When is it happening?" Bessie asked

"On the twenty ninth. It'll be a private ceremony at St. Michael's. Alex and I will be witnesses."

"How can they keep the ceremony private if it's in a church?" Pie wondered.

I shrugged. "Well, as private as they can keep it. People may wander into the church for one reason or another, but since no one will be invited, for all intents and purposes, it will be private."

"Where are they planning to live?" Bessie devours marital news with her meals.

Alex answered. "For now, in Jeanne's little house in Bella Villa but it's too small for the long haul. Particularly if Chrissie lives with them until she can afford a place of her own. They're planning to build around here as soon as they find suitable land. Jim said that there are a few appropriate sites on the market. The problem will be finding a site where it won't be too expensive to drill for water."

Bessie the genius said, "Can't Chrissie stay in your cabin during the week? It's empty then, isn't it?"

Alex and I looked at one another. "If it's okay with the Cokers, it's okay with us."

We checked with the Cokers. It was okay with them, too.

CHAPTER 4

May 24, 1993

As we emerged from the cabin, we saw Gertie pacing up to her fence. Alex went to commune with her and they engaged in an interminable conversation. After a while, they finally said their good-byes and Alex joined me at the Mustang. He slid into the passenger seat.

"What could you possibly be saying to an alpaca for such a long time?"

"We were laying out her agenda for the week. What do you talk to that clunker about?"

"Mostly I'm threatening to take the damn thing to the wreckers."

By this time we had reached the end of the driveway. I looked right and spied a green tractor crawling towards us. It was towing a cultivator that was blocking both lanes. Alex spied the same thing.

"Well," he said, "we might as well make the most of it."

We unbuckled our seat belts and settled in for a snoggle. Eventually, there was a tap on the window. There was Claudia Coker, barely suppressing a laugh. "That cultivator's been past for quite a while. Do you think you might move your car and let us out?"

"Geez, Claudia," Alex said, "we're sorry. We'll move right

now."

"That's alright, Alex. Daryl and I were enjoying the scene, but it was starting to repeat itself."

She went back to her car and I pulled onto the road.

D'ya have a line?"

"Indeed, I do," I said. *"A young math'matician named Clive"*

"No, you don't. I had a mathematician last time."

"So? Your mathematician isn't the only one in the world. Continue, please."

"I still think it's cheating. *Was lucky to just be alive*"

"You didn't give me much to go on."

Alex sneered. "You didn't deserve much. Stealing my mathematician like that."

"Sorehead. *His boozing most brash, caused his hard disk to crash*"

We continued down the road a bit. I said, "You give up? I get to pick the restaurant."

Alex frowned. "You're going to pick R.T's aren't you? Even knowing that I don't like Cajun."

"Then come up with something. We're almost to LIT."

Finally, *"The guy shouldn't drink and derive."*

I burst out laughing. "I gotta admit it. Well done, husband."

Alex grinned. "I was desperate."

I pulled into the parking place and addressed the jury.

"A young math'matician named Clive
Was lucky to just be alive

His boozing, most brash
Caused his hard disk to crash,
The guy shouldn't drink and derive"
No question. Cheers and huzzahs.

Don and I walked down the admin corridor. "What's new on the remodeling front, Don?

Don laughed. "You know we're putting a whirlpool tub in the remodeled basement?"

"Connie told me. I may borrow it."

"The plumber we got is a great, big, fat, guy. He stands about six feet and must top three hundred pounds. In order to get all of the pipes in, they had to excavate a big hole. So the plumber gets in the hole and has to stretch flat on his back in order to do whatever the hell plumbers do. Now, the hole is a pretty snug fit. There's not a lot of wiggle room. Anyway, he gets finished and then he can't get out.

"The rest of the contracting crew try to pull him out but they can't budge him. And they don't want to chip away at the walls of the hole because they're afraid they'll damage him."

"What did they finally do?" I asked. "Or is the guy still there? Maybe they should leave him there and not feed him until he loses weight."

"They probably didn't think of that. They called the fire department. Once they stopped laughing, the firemen gave him a rope to hang onto and they hauled him up with the rope. He was one cheesed off plumber."

I turned into my office. Ben and Chuck were seated there. Ben said, "News from the gay hot wire."

"K-k-kind of hard to get the narrative in order," Chuck said, "but let's start with the occupation of Adam Brattice's brother, Howard. He's Counselor to the mob."

Ben continued, "That means he would know that Cody Kletsch has a nasty gambling habit and is in deep to the bad guys."

That threw me. "Really! I would never have guessed."

"W-w-wait. There's more. Adam Brattice's wife has been having a long-running affair with Counselor Howard."

I produced a smug smile. "I knew that."

They stared at me. "How did you find that out?" Ben asked.

"I have my sources." Then took pity on them. "Adam's sister told Paul Richards at the Forensic Lab. But interesting as it is, Howard's extra-curricular activities are, I think, irrelevant. However, it's a pretty good guess that you've identified the thief. Cody must be frantic for money."

Ben and Chuck arose. As they left, Ben remarked, "Thievery most vial."

I walked to Pie's office for our usual morning meeting. Don was already there. I clued them in on the fresh revelations.

"How do you discover these things?" Don asked.

"Ben and Chuck both frequent a gay bar and..."

"Are they lovers?" Don interrupted.

"What's that got to do with anything? But since you ask, no. Just friends."

"How do you know that?"

"Don! Stop interrupting."

Don subsided.

"Another patron of the bar is a mafioso and..."

"In a gay bar? You're kidding!" Don was incorrigible.

"Yes, in a gay bar. Ben says he swings both ways. If you'll stop interrupting, I'll answer your first question."

Pie, who was vainly trying to follow the conversation, said "What *was* the first question?"

"Don asked how I find these things out. Apparently, Ben or Chuck mentioned that I was on loan to the Forensic Lab and the mafioso told them about Cody's gambling addiction, Howard Brattice's connection to the mob, and that he was playing around with Adam Brattice's wife. I guess *omerta* doesn't apply in this situation."

"Huh. So it looks like Kletsch is the reagent *gonif*. Do you think Richards will send you home?"

"I hope so, but it isn't certain that Kletsch is the *gonif*. Paul may want me to stick around until it's proven."

"Well," said Don, "I don't know what else you can do unless he wants you to beat a confession out of the guy."

Jim Daly intercepted me before I could get out of the building. He looked mightily pleased with himself. "That's great that Chrissie can use the cabin during the week. It was gonna be a squeeze in Jeanne's little house."

"Glad to be of service."

"Transportation was going to be a problem, but I got a really good price on a 1990 Taurus. Chrissie's birthday is next month so I'll give it to her in advance. She's excited."

"You're a good daddy, Jim. Next to Santa Claus, the best."

Ben had walked up during the conversation. "Do you know," he asked, "what Santa Claus calls his elves?"

"What?" Jim asked.

"Subordinate Clauses." Ben went on his way.

"Outstanding," Jim said. "I've got a middle school tour in ten minutes. I'll use it on them."

He went off to get his Einstein mask.

The clunker was in a conciliatory mood and we made it to the Forensic Lab in good order. I stopped at the desk to pick up my schedule for the day, but Cody had not left it. I found Paul in his office. He beamed. "Good Monday, Bea. Have you found the culprit yet?"

"Maybe." I told him about Cody's unfortunate debt to the mob.

Paul was no longer beaming. He leaned back. Ruffled his white hair. Scratched his mustache. Stroked his goatee. "I guess we can't put paid until I confront him."

I nodded.

"Well, it'll have to wait. Cody hasn't come in yet. He came in late Sunday and compared the kid's DNA with Adam's and left me a note. Adam is the father, much to Ms. Hunter's chagrin. I called her first thing this morning.

"Cody worked pretty late on the Brattice tests and I guess he decided he deserved some time off. He hasn't called in, so he's probably sleeping the sleep of the dead. Suppose you do the interviews with the rest of the staff and then we can decide where to go from there."

The 'management audit' interviews went, for the most part, stultifyingly well. The staff described their jobs, and the relationship of their jobs to everyone else's jobs. Cody, as supervisor, assigns cases to Jazz and provides whatever help is needed. He also testifies before the Court in high profile cases. Jazz, the analyst, oversees and directs the techies. She's involved in quality control from start to finish, does lab work, writes reports, and is generally the fulcrum around which the team revolves. The techies are the grunts. They don't do any data analysis, but they do everything else, including ordering reagents and other supplies.

They all think that Paul is a fine director. They all think that Cody is a good supervisor. They all love working for the Forensic Lab. Since the audit was only a cover story, I didn't press them. Danielson alone had something interesting to say and it certainly made up for the boredom induced by the other two.

The interview began with Danielson clearing her throat. "I started to say something last time, Bea, but I really didn't want to go on. It was too painful. I thought it over and I think I should tell you. If you dug, you'd probably find out anyway."

I looked at her expectantly.

"I suppose you know that everyone who works here has their DNA on record. Most labs didn't do that until a couple of years ago, but Paul, bless his persnickety hide, demanded it even before the FBI started. We do that so if, God forbid, some sample gets contaminated, we can find out where the contamination came from. Then we can talk to the contaminator and maybe give him some retraining.

"Well, some time ago, before I started working here, my brother, George, worked here and so his DNA is in the archives. Before he went back to school and got his advanced degree, he was a fireman with citations for bravery. Sometimes on week-ends he volunteered to feed the homeless. Then he had a heart attack and died. He was a wonderful man and Minnie, his daughter, my niece, worshipped him. I think in honor of George, she worked here one summer as an unpaid intern. So her DNA is also in the archives. I can understand why she took the unpaid job. I'm also here because of George."

She produced a wry smile. "Of course, I'm getting paid, pittance though it is.

"Well, Cody was fooling around in the lab one weekend and compared Minnie's and George's DNA. George wasn't her father. Cody went to George's widow and told her that if she didn't give him money, he'd tell Minnie. She didn't believe he'd do it so she didn't give him any. And he did tell Minnie. And Minnie committed suicide. Her mother committed suicide, too. Before she did, she mailed a note to me telling all."

I was stunned. "Didn't you tell anyone what Cody had done?"

"Of course not! After all I went through with George's death and two suicides, I certainly didn't want to get embroiled in a scandal."

"So you just let Cody go on blackmailing people."

"Oh, the only other person he could blackmail was Elliott Giles and that overbearing southern snob has it coming."

"I see. And may I ask what he did to Elliott?"

Danielson giggled. "Well, everyone knows how proud Elliott is of his 'Vuhginya' heritage. 'Mah lineage goes back to a foundah. None othah than Mistah James Madison.' Well, Cody ran his DNA and discovered that the proud descendent of Mr. Madison has a touch of the tarbrush! That kind of testing couldn't have been done anyplace except here or the FBI or a couple of private labs. It was Elliott's bad luck that both the capability and Cody were here.

"Cody told me, but I've kept my mouth shut. Heaven knows, I don't want to be responsible for another suicide. But I bet Elliott is paying through the nostrils."

I sat there looking at Danielson. Cody could go on blackmailing people forever, leaving misery in his wake, and this sanctimonious slug was worried about being touched by a scandal. I was going to have to tell Paul.

I thanked Danielson for her time and left.

I returned to Paul's office to find that Cody still wasn't in.

"I'm not sure that this is relevant to my task, but since it does increase the likelihood that Cody's the thief, I think the information should be thrown into the pot." I produced the information.

Paul kept shaking his head. Finally he said, "My conversation with Cody will go on longer than I anticipated."

Pie and Don were appropriately horrified. "*Gottenyu*" Pie lamented. "A whole team full of *paskudniks*!"

"Well, not the whole team," I pointed out. "Jazz Nishiyama seems like a good person."

"Yeah," Don said. "That's what you said about Cody."

Pie alertly changed the subject. "Is this the night you're

going to the retirement dinner?"

"Yep. Chrissie's driving there with Molly and Ralph. Alex will stay with Jim Daly in the District. After the dinner, I'll take Chrissie to Jim's and pick up Alex. I'm gonna enjoy that ride with Chrissie!"

The dinner was a hoot. About forty people were there and at least half of them had been let in on the joke, thanks to Ralph Manley. The other half had been informed by their tablemates. Even Ken Austin, the esteemed honoree, was *au courant*. Molly and Chrissie alone were clueless.

The Fire Pit had been commandeered for the event. The restaurant had set up a head table at which sat Austin, his wife, his three offspring, and Molly. The rest of us were at regular tables, each seating four to six people. I was at a table for four – me, Ralph, the very pregnant Dr. Adrienne Hodler and her husband. He was there to rush her to the hospital in case the baby wanted to come out and join the party. Waiters bustled about serving food and drink. Adrienne eschewed the alcohol. Ralph snuck the wide mouthed jar under the table. Adrienne volunteered to do the pouring, since Molly was unlikely to suspect her of collusion. Unfortunately, after a bit of experimentation, we determined that she couldn't bend over that far. After further discussion, we decided that Ralph would do the pouring. Molly wouldn't notice him, either.

Every time I saw Molly looking at me, I hailed a waiter and ordered a bourbon, placing the glass between me and Ralph. When Molly looked away, Ralph would pick up the glass and pour it into the jar, returning the empty glass to the table.

Adrienne added a new wrinkle. "Pregnant women need to pee a lot. Why doesn't Bea accompany me to the ladies room when I have to go. She can kind of lean on me and wobble a little. Molly will probably think I'm taking her to throw up."

Excellent idea. It was implemented.

All this went on through dinner, several appreciative good-bye speeches, the presentation of the good-bye gift (a heavy gold letter opener) and finally Austin's farewell talk. Every once in a while, during his speech, Austin would pretend to be annoyed and would glare at our table. Molly was looking increasingly distressed. Chrissie looked frantic.

Ultimately, the evening ended. Ralph and the Hodlers went to present Austin with the bourbon-filled jar as an impromptu additional retirement present. I went to find Chrissie. She was huddled with Molly, who said to me, "You can't drive in that condition, Bea. Give Chrissie the car keys."

"Why?"

"Because you're shit-faced, that's why."

All innocence. "Me? I haven't had anything alcoholic to drink all night."

Molly and Chrissie goggled at me as the realization dawned that they'd been had. Molly muttered, "I'll get you for this," and stalked off.

"Come on Chrissie, let's go."

The weather was gorgeous, the top was down and Chrissie was laughing. "What did you do with all of the drinks you ordered. We thought we might have to carry you out to the car."

"We had a jar hidden under the table and Ralph poured the drinks into it as they came. He gave the jar to Austin as a farewell gift."

Chrissie giggled. "So now *he* can get shit-faced."

As we passed the LIT building, Chrissie asked, "What are you doing at the Forensic Lab? Daddy said you've been spending time there."

"It's an interesting assignment. Someone is stealing reagents needed for DNA analysis and they want me to pretend I'm doing a management audit. They think that during the interviews I might be able to get a clue to the thief."

"How's it going?"

"I think we're closing in."

Chrissie thought for a bit. "Our lab doesn't do any DNA stuff. I wish we did; I'd like to learn more about plant fingerprinting."

I nodded. "We don't have the resources to maintain that kind of facility. Would you like me to see if the Forensic Lab would take you on as a summer intern?"

Chrissie pondered. Then, "No. No thanks. I know I'm going to have to expand my areas of knowledge but I'm learning so much from Dr. Manley and Dr. Cameron now that I'll wait until graduate school before I see which way I want to go. I really love it at LIT."

We were approaching the Bella Villa turnoff when we noticed an ancient station wagon with its hood up and a stocky Black guy standing there looking distressed. I pulled over.

"Can we give you a lift to a garage?"

"Yes. No. I don't know. This is a mess."

"What's the problem?" Chrissie asked. "Aside from the dead car, I mean."

"My bass fiddle is in the wagon and I'm due at the club in an hour. There's no way I can make it."

"How big is the instrument?" I asked.

The guy looked at me as if I were from outer space. "The size of a bass fiddle," he said.

"Don't be a smartass," Chrissie said.

I said, "Will it fit in the Mustang if we keep the top down?"

He brightened. "Yeah. That'll work." Then he deflated. "But I gotta get into DC."

"That's where we're going," Chrissie said. "Let's get it loaded."

We were struggling with the fiddle when a County Sheriff's car pulled up. A deputy got out. The Black guy looked alarmed.

"Hello, Walt," I said.

"Hello, Dr. Goode. You got trouble?" he asked.

"We're trying to get this thing out of the wagon and into the Mustang. His car is stalled and he needs to get to his job."

Walt walked over to the wagon. "Him and me can muscle it in if you and Chrissie get out of the way." He approached the Black guy and stuck out his hand. "I'm Walt Avery."

The Black guy looked startled, but took the hand. "I'm Lomas Hopper." They shook. Then they transferred the fiddle to the Mustang.

Walt said, "I'll get the car towed to the Department." He turned to Hopper. "We won't charge. I been wanting to take a look at the inside of one of those antiques."

"Walt," I asked, "are you going in now?"

"Yeah. Why?"

"Could you call Jim Daly and Mr. Hopper's club and explain that we'll be late?"

We gave him the phone numbers and got in the Mustang.

"Hey," Walt called, "pick up the car tomorrow afternoon. It'll be in the sheriff's parking space. I'll call your club and leave a message if it's not ready. Check before you come."

Introductions were made as I pulled out. I'm Beatrice Goode. I'm Christine Daly. I'm Lomas Hopper. Call me Bea, Chrissie, and Lomas respectively.

As we drove down the country road, we debated the route that we would take into the District. Toss-up between Georgia Avenue and Sixteenth Street, finally deciding on the former. The north end of Georgia is in Silver Spring where a lot of building is going on. The National Oceanographic and Atmospheric Administration's new complex is nearby as well as any number of retail businesses. Crisfield's Seafood is a landmark. We shortly passed the rather ordinary neighborhood around Walter Reed Hospital but as soon as we left the hospital's orbit we traveled through a boarded-up, drug-infested stretch until we got to the area around Howard University, where things calmed down again.

I acted as chauffeur while Chrissie turned to the backseat and discussed jazz with Lomas. Eavesdropping, I discovered that Lomas played with a trio at a club in the Shaw section of DC – part of the DC ghetto. Lomas's trio was not just any old trio. He was the leader and played bass. Arthur Burbank was the drummer. Willis

Rockwell played the sax and sometimes sang. Lomas had gone to
Washington's Duke Ellington School of the Arts where he not only
received his high school education, but learned his craft – a learning
experience that included some classical training. Every evening the
three budding musicians would meet and Lomas would pass on what
he had learned that day. The other two would adapt that knowledge
to their own instruments.

I butted in to the conversation. "Does your group have a
name?"

"Yeah. *We Three and Whatever.*"

I butted back out.

"So what kind of music do you play?" Chrissie asked.

"We do everything. Except hip hop. We don't do hip hop.
Or go go. We no go go. You know Bobby McFerrin?"

"Sure. He did *Don't Worry, Be Happy.* And now he's doing
some great vocal stuff."

Lomas was enthusiastic. "That's him. We wanna be like
him. Not the vocal stuff, nobody can do Bobby's vocal stuff but
Bobby. But we want his attitude. He doesn't let anything limit him.
Did you know his dad was an opera singer? That's where he got that
attitude. We want a piece of the attitude. We wanna do Dixie and
we wanna do hot jazz and cool jazz, maybe even some be-bop but
we haven't tried that yet. Haven't tried hard rock either. Hard to do
with our instruments and probably not worth it, anyway. We wanna
do a little Brahms for bass, drums, and sax. We wanna do
everything.

"Hey, can you stay for our gig tonight?"

"I don't think so," Chrissie said. "We have to go to work

tomorrow."

"The *Whatever* part of the group is singing in the first number. Can you stay for that?"

I re-butted in. "Yes."

While I was in the butting mode, I asked Lomas what his day job was.

"I teach music at the 'hood's high school. I wanted to teach music in the 'hood so as soon as I graduated from Ellington I enrolled at UDC and got my education degree. Did it in three years," he said proudly. "It wasn't hard to get placed because no one else wants to teach in the 'hood."

"How come you want to?" Chrissie asked.

"Because," Lomas answered, "it's the only place where I have a chance to change some kids' lives."

"Have you changed any lives yet?"

Lomas grinned at Chrissie. "One of my kids just got a scholarship to Julliard. I think, if it hadn't been for music, he might be in jail now. Or dead."

"That's great," Chrissie said. "Do the other guys teach, too?"

"No," Lomas said. "My folks were the only ones who could afford to send a kid to college. The tuition is over $800 and that doesn't count other things like books. Willis's mom belongs to the fu – whoops – lover-of-the-month club. He doesn't know who his dad is. And Arthur's father is a junkie and in jail. Come to think of it, if it weren't for music Willis and Arthur might be in jail, too. Or dead.

"Willis drives a pizza delivery truck. Arthur works in the Hilton uptown. He carries suitcases to the rooms. Tips aren't bad.

"Do you you know anything about the Shaw neighborhood?" Chrissie and I disclaimed all knowledge.

"Well," said Lomas, "It's taken a long time to recover from the '68 riots, but we're starting to get gentrified. The block we're on, though, wasn't much touched by the riots and it's still a working class neighborhood. Some brownstones, row houses, an apartment building with students from Howard living in it. Elementary school's a few blocks away, so kiddies are playing in the street long after they should have been in bed. Parents are usually sitting on the front stoop watching them. Shaw has a fascinating history. Started as freed slave encampments...."

"Hey, Bea," he interrupted himself, "we're coming into Shaw. Take a right on Florida past the construction and those Ethiopian restaurants. Then take a left on U, past the Prince Hall Masonic Temple, to Eleventh. Lees Flower Shop is on the corner. The club is there as soon as you turn, on the right side of the block. There's a mom and pop grocery across the street."

The street was an unprepossessing residential block, with a lone double storefront on the right hand corner. I pulled up and parked. The storefront windows were painted black. A white, hand-painted sign announced 'WE THREE & WHATEVER". The sidewalk was covered with about twenty standing people. A mighty cheer greeted us. Lomas jumped out of the car and directed the removal of his fiddle. He informed the crowd that his saviors would stay for the first number. Two members of the throng volunteered to remain outside to guard the Mustang. One of them said to me, "If we not here, your wheels be jacked before the first riff."

We, along with the rest of the crowd, entered the club, where

Lomas introduced us to Arthur and Willis, the other members of the trio. We all shook hands and they ascended three steps to a little stage, illuminated by a spotlight. They started to tune up.

The room held about fifty people, all of them Black, ranging in age from teens to elderly. There was a bar at the back of the room. A waiter directed us to one of the few tables that had empty seats. We joined a good-looking couple in their late thirties or early forties. The lone male at the table asked, "Can I get you ladies a drink?"

Chrissie responded seriously, "No thank you. I think she's had quite enough this evening."

I'm going to kill that kid.

I turned to our tablemates and said, "I'm Bea, and this is Chrissie."

The woman responded. "I'm Glenna and that's Al." There was a flurry of arms across the table as we shook hands.

"How you come to know Lomas?" Al asked.

Chrissie explained about finding him stranded in the wilds of Maryland and delivering him to the club. "We can only stay for the first number. My dad will really worry if I don't get home soon."

Glenna said, "We're real grateful you got him here. This is the best of the music around. Some of the places just have kids who do hip hop or go go. Some of the other places have good musicians but you always know what'll be goin' down. No surprises."

"Yeah," Al agreed. "They be straight jazz guys. Some of them build their own thing. Some of them follow Coltrane or Davis. But here, we don't know what we gonna get except it'll be good.

One time they even played Mozart. Never thought I'd like Mozart but it was great. Anyway, this place is the most fun.

"An' the three of them, they good guys. Not into drugs or nothin'. Willis is the odd one. He part Cherokee. We kid him about being half breed."

Glenna went back to the earlier theme. "Lomas woulda been here on time but his brother does some farming in that Black section up north in Maryland and one of his nephews was being five today so Lomas went up to play the fiddle for his birthday party."

Al jerked his head toward Chrissie. "It was real nice of your mama to rescue Lomas. We'da been mightily disappointed if the trio couldn't go on."

Chrissie giggled. "Yeah, she's okay. But she's not my mother, she's my boss's boss."

I don't think Molly would agree with that description.

"My gracious," the woman said, "how come you're traveling with someone that high up?"

I entered the conversation. "The kid needs someone senior to make sure she stays out of trouble."

They both stared at me and then started to laugh."

Glenna asked, "You know what the *Whatever* in *We Three and Whatever* stands for?"

We both shook our heads.

"Well, the *Whatever* part of the name is a few different women. We rotate nights singing a couple of numbers with the group. Tonight, it's Arthur's wife, Michelle. I'm on next week."

Al said, "Those two run a kiddie care center. They partners. They classy ladies."

"Are you and Michelle the only *Whatevers*?"

"No," Glenna answered. "Flo is the other *Whatever*. She's a dressmaker. Makes the clothes we perform in. In fact, here she is now."

A small, tawny-colored woman walked over and sat down in one of the vacant chairs. Glenna said, "This is the other *Whatever*. Flo, this is Chrissie and Bea."

Al stood up. "I think I better go to the little boys room before they start."

Glenna stood up. "Good idea. You all want to come?"

We all shook our heads.

Flo was garbed in a beautifully tailored, muted blue suit over a cream blouse. Chrissie was staring at the woman. Finally she said, "Your suit is lovely. It looks like a Florence Barney."

Flo smiled. "That's not surprising. It *is* a Florence Barney and *I'm* Florence Barney. Thank you for rescuing Lomas."

I was amazed. Fashion is not my thing. But even I know that Florence Barney and Ralph Lauren are the royalty of American fashion designers – whatever Oscar de la Renta may think. I turned to the Royal. "And you are a *Whatever*?"

"Lomas and I went to Duke Ellington together. I started out in the Music track as he did, but it was clear that while I might become a very good singer, I was never going to be great. And I wanted to be great. I still do."

Chrissie interjected, "You certainly achieved your ambition."

"Thank you. I shifted to Art, took the requisite courses and enjoyed myself enormously. But again, greatness did not beckon. In my senior year, I started sketching fashion. And the more I looked at my sketches, the more I thought that this was my path. I applied to the Rhode Island School of Design. Sent my portfolio. They not only accepted me, they offered a full tuition scholarship. It's a marvelous school!"

I asked, "Did you apprentice at a studio when you graduated?"

Florence laughed. "No. I was funded to start my own label in my own studio. My angels also arranged the marketing necessary to launch my career." She thought a minute. "They've made their money back."

"Who were your angels?" Chrissie asked.

Florence laughed again. "They insist on anonymity. But I can tell you one thing about them. All three of them made their money playing football."

Chrissie and I stared at her. "Are you putting us on?" I asked.

"Not at all."

Chrissie said, "And you join *We Three* on weekends?"

"These are my roots, Chrissie. Just as they are Lomas's. He could be anything he wants. Classical, jazz, anything. He's that good. But when all is said and done, this is where we belong."

I remarked, "Glenna said you were a dressmaker."

Flo giggled. "At least she didn't call me a seamstress. But it's better that way. I don't wish to make people uncomfortable. You know. I help Lomas with the Foundation and I fund the Rhode Island School of Design to give scholarships to talented kids from the Black ghettos. But I keep my head down."

Glenna and Al returned and sat down.

Al said, "Final offer. Anyone want me to get you a drink before they start?"

Three "No thanks."

The mic popped into action. Lomas announced that *Whatever* would do the first number. One of the classy ladies came out of the audience, walked up the stairs, and gave Lomas a peck on the cheek. He went back to his fiddle.

Michelle is a tall, good-looking woman. A spectacular floor-length burgundy sheath covered her ample but not overly-ample frame. She said, "Good evening."

Arthur raised his sticks and the traps emitted a discreet rhythm. Lomas picked it up on the plucked fiddle. Then Willis' sax gave a low growl. And finally, Michelle belted "One scotch..."

The audience erupted in applause. Michelle laughed, stopped her belting, and shushed them. It took a bit, but they shushed.

She began again, "One scotch, one bourbon, one beer,

               One scotch, one bourbon, one beer,

               Please Mr. Bartender, come here...."

Chrissie and I both leaned forward. That classy lady was incredibly good. She paused to give the trio space for some riffs. They were as good as any I'd ever heard play. Michelle reclaimed the mic for one last turn. Chrissie and I were pounding our palms so hard we didn't notice Lomas arriving.

"We have to pick up my car tomorrow. Can you give me directions to the sheriff's office? Arthur can take me there."

I nodded. "But if you can meet me around five on the road near where we picked you up, it might be easier if I just led you there."

Lomas nodded. "Sounds good. Are you sure you can't stay for a few more numbers?"

"We'd love to. But I think I'd better get Chrissie home and pick up my husband."

"Understand. Listen, I can't thank you enough for..."

"The trio and Michelle were more than adequate payment. Your group is fantastic."

Lomas beamed and beckoned to a couple of young men. "Jase," he said to one of them, "get your car and lead our benefactors out of the 'hood. Jordan, you ride shotgun."

We said good-bye to our tablemates and followed Jordan out the door. We released the two men who were doing guard duty and entered the Mustang, Jordan in the back seat. Jason arrived in a souped up Chevy and led us to Capitol Hill, where Jordan transferred to the Chevy.

As we moved off, Chrissie turned to me. "What players do you think bankrolled Ms. Barney? Pretty sure to be Redskins."

I agreed. "Lots of good guys on that team. Daryl Green do you think?"

"Maybe Art Monk," said Chrissie. "Could be any three of the Black players. Brian Mitchell?"

"How about Charles Mann? Well, we may never know."

Chrissie said, "Why do you think they want to be anonymous?"

I laughed. "Do you think those macho guys want to be publicly associated with the designer fashion industry? They'd never live it down."

We drove the few blocks to Jim's place. It was in another world.

CHAPTER 5
May 25, 1993

I went out to get the paper while Alex poured the last of the breakfast coffee. Opening the front door, I noticed two interesting things. The first was a moving truck. Two big guys were preparing to lug furniture into the house next door. A black Cadillac deVille was just pulling in behind them, blocking the Mustang. A couple got out of the car. The man was five foot seven or eight, powerfully built, black hair and, from what I could see from above, getting a little bald on top.

He inspected the terrain and called up, "Hey, we blockin' ya from gettin' out?"

Now that was an improvement. "We're okay for the next ten minutes or so. Then if you can let our Mustang out, the parking place will be free for the rest of the day."

"'At's good." He walked up our steps and introduced himself. "I'm Johnny Notte." He pointed at the woman who was giving instructions to the movers. "At's Marilyn. My bettah half."

Marilyn was nearly Johnny's height, short bottle-blonde hair, knock-out figure. Both she and Johnny looked as if they spent time working out. That surmise was verified as the movers began unloading some impressive exercise equipment.

"I'm Bea Goode. My husband, Alex, is inside."

Johnny looked alarmed. "You're Bea Goode? You ain't

Ben's boss are ya?"

Uh oh. "Yes, I am. And you're Ben's and Chuck's friend."

"Oh, geez. You ain't gonna tell..."

I made a shushing noise as Marilyn approached. "No, of course not."

Marilyn said, "Johnny, go tell the movers where to put the tv."

Johnny ran down the stairs.

Marilyn smiled, "Don't worry about it. I know. Johnny doesn't know I know so that's okay. I don't really care, as long as he treats me good.

"What's that thing on your stoop?"

"That thing" was the second item of interest. A dead rat, its unlovely carcass caked in blood. A note was pinned to its neck.

Alex came out the door as Johnny was running up the steps. Marilyn pointed at the rat.

Alex and Johnny, in unison. "What the hell!"

They both bent down to read the note, nearly bumping heads.

The note said, "Back off."

"Back off what?" Alex and Johnny asked, still in unison.

"No clue. Last week it might have been telling me to stop trying to find the reagent thief, but we've probably already found the guy. Have *you* irritated someone?" I asked Alex.

"No one I can think of, unless it's the sonuvabitch who just moved out. Or maybe the mob. Maybe it was meant for the sonuvabitch and when the delivery boy saw the empty house he just dumped it on the nearest doorstep."

I peered at the rat.

"Don't touch it," Alex said.

"I wouldn't dream of touching it. It's gross!"

"I'm going to call the cops," Alex said and turned to go inside.

"Don' call cops," Johnny said. "I'll take care a it. But I can tellya one t'ing." He smiled, "It wasn' da sonuvabitch an' it wasn' da mob."

Alex looked at him. "How do you know that?"

I answered. "Uh, Alex. This is Johnny Notte, Ben's and Chuck's friend."

It took Alex a minute before it registered. "Oh."

Johnny explained. "Look. My boss," he chuckled, "who is da sonuvabitch's boss too, wants him in New Yawk an' wants me heah to take care a t'ings. You know, keep t'ings quiet. We ain' gonna dump no rat on a citizen's stoop. 'Specially a citizen dat lives nex' door."

Alex's mouth dropped. "You mean the sonuvabitch is Mafia?"

Johnny laughed, "You said it, I didn'. Anyway, I'll fin' out who done it. Like I said, I'll take care a it."

Marilyn said, "I'll get something to wrap the damn thing. The movers'll have something." She headed for the movers.

Alex said to Johnny, "Glad to have you next door."

Johnny bowed. "Same ta you." He went back down to join Marilyn and the movers.

Alex and I went back in the house. The coffee was cold. Well, sometimes life throws you a curve.

"On a more mundane level," I asked, "may I raid the freezer

86

for a large amount of your assorted cookies?"

"Sure," Alex said, "But why?"

"I'd like to bring them to the BioCenter as expiation for disrupting the retirement dinner."

"You mean you'd like to make peace with Molly."

"That too."

He got up to load the dishwasher while I raided the freezer.

It was another gorgeous spring day. In fact, there had been a long line of gorgeous spring days except for a few drizzles here and there. If we didn't get a good rain soon, the farmers were going to be in trouble.

I grabbed the shopping bag full of cookies and we once more left the house. Johnny had moved his car and the Mustang awaited. I slid into the passenger seat as Alex started the motor. He pulled out.

He remarked, "Our new neighbors will certainly be different."

"Indeed. And it's a good bet that Johnny gets his snow shoveled. What do you think he does for the mob?"

Alex said, "I don't think I want to know."

On reflection, I agreed with him.

After a bit Alex said, "Bea, maybe we should be gentle with the limerick today. You know, cooperate."

"How come?"

Alex explained, "Well, you must be a little unnerved by that rat. I don't want to stress you."

"I'm not unnerved. I'm pissed off. Hit me with the first

line".

"Okay. But here's a gentle one. Even if you aren't unnerved, *I* am. *A guy with the brains of a gnat"*

"This is your idea of gentle?"

Alex was indignant. "What did you want? See Dick run?"

"That wouldn't scan. Okay, take this" *Said, I don't know where I am at,*

"Way to go. Fast ball right in my wheelhouse." He grinned.

" I don't think that I'm here,

Who knows where I'll appear?

"Finish it off, babe."

"As you wish. *Ah! I must be Schrodinger's cat.*"

"That's not bad," Alex said. "That's worth at least two hips and a hooray."

After an appreciable amount of braking and swearing, Alex left the Interstate for the decorous climb to LIT. Some workers were sprucing up the shed where the Alligator Wrestling Emporium once was. Other workers were leveling the parking lot. An asphalt paving machine was standing by.

"Do you think the alligator place is returning?" I asked.

"Doubt it," Alex said. "The guy left under a cloud. A restaurant maybe? Or a souvenir shop? How about a porno store?"

I frowned at him. "You shoulda stopped with the souvenir shop. In any case, it's a good location for something," I said. "Maybe they're just gussying it up to attract a buyer."

We continued past the whatever-it's-gonna-be and loafed up the road, admiring the blooming fruit trees and the wild flowers that lined the road. Spring is a lovely season anywhere, but it's particularly lovely in the country. Native azaleas were in profusion. Coreopsis, bleeding heart, columbines, yarrow. Not even an early morning rat could spoil it.

Alex pulled into the LIT lot and greeted the multitude.

> *"A guy with the brains of a gnat*
> *Said, I don't know where I am at,*
> *I don't think that I'm here,*
> *Who knows where I'll appear?*
> *Ah! I must be Schrodinger's cat."*

The multitude went into its huddle. They huddled and huddled. Voices were raised. There seemed to be some kind of conflict going on. Finally, Don was disgorged from the group.

"There is no doubt," he said, "that this is a very fine limerick. Everyone agreed on that."

Alex and I looked at one another. So what was the problem?

"However," Don went on, "this is the third consecutive limerick dealing with mathematics or a neighboring subject."

Aha!

"There is also no doubt that mathematics is a respectable, ancient, discipline."

Well, I should hope that no one doubts that.

"Nonetheless," my colleague continued, "the biologists are restive. They feel discriminated against, and on examination of the evidence, it appears that they have cause. We therefore respectfully request that in the interest of fair play, you knock off the math for a while."

Alex and I thought this over. "Ya think?" he said.

"Why not?" I answered.

And so, in order to promote peace and amity within the Federal government, we agreed to knock off the math for a while.

Alex went off toward the Computer Sciences Center, Don and I toward the admin wing.

"How's the remodeling going, Don?"

Don shook his head. "You're not going to believe this one."

"Sure I will."

"The contractors were staying late and were upstairs working on the floors. They were mostly sanding, but replacing the hardwood in some spots. Connie and I were eating dinner. In the middle of dessert, there was a loud noise and one of the workmen came crashing through the ceiling. Landed about three feet from us."

"Good heavens! Is he okay?"

"Yeah, shaken up a little but otherwise okay."

Ben, who had come up behind us, said, "Don't you just hate it when people drop in at dinner time?"

He trundled past.

We chose to ignore him.

"You're late this morning. You and Alex felt the need for an extra snoggle?"

"Whatever we may have felt, that's not what caused the delay. We were delayed by a dirty rat and a friendly mafioso."

I recounted the morning's events to Don.

"Good God. That rat still looks like a warning from the Mafia. Is your gangster neighbor sure it isn't? What have you been doing at the Forensic Lab?"

"He should know. And I'm not doing anything at the

Forensic Lab. We've fingered the likely thief, so there'd be no reason to warn me off. My job there is done. Besides, who's to say that the warning is for me? It could be aimed at Alex, except why would the Mafia want to stop him from doing computer research? I don't think it was the mob. But maybe someone who wanted it to look like the mob left it on the wrong doorstep."

We paused in front of my office. "That doesn't sound reasonable," Don said.

"To quote Arthur Conan Doyle, 'Once you have eliminated the impossible, whatever remains, however improbable, must be true'."

"So," asked Don, "if three or four contradictory things remain, they must all be true?"

"Hmmm. Let me try another quote. 'Sometimes I've believed as many as six impossible things before breakfast.' Oh, nuts!"

"Now, what?" Don asked.

"I forgot the BioCenter's cookies. I gotta go back to the car and get them."

"You got cookies?"

"I will have once I get them from the Mustang. I'll bring some to Pie's office when I give you the recap of Ken Austin's retirement party."

Don moseyed on while I retrieved the big bag of cookies and extracted a little bag for the Director's office. Alex need never know.

My phone was ringing when I got back to my office. It was

Freddy Langsteth, an Office of Management and Budget analyst and a friend of mine and Alex. "Bea, we're set to visit you guys in June and we've been getting buzzed by Congressman Bowlden and..."

"...he has a Very *Very* Important Constituent," I finished for her.

Freddy laughed. "The man has a diligent aide. Can I get an off-the-record briefing about your BioCenter?"

"Sure. Do you want to meet or just talk on the phone?"

Freddy thought. "Can we meet someplace obscure near your place for lunch? No rule against it, but if we're spotted together some eyebrows might be raised, since I'm one of the analysts assigned to the LIT briefing."

No one who knows Freddy Langsteth would even dream that she'd be influenced by anything but facts. However, not everyone knows Freddy Langsteth and those eyebrows might very well ascend.. I said, "Do you know where the Fire Pit is?"

Freddy knew the location and we agreed to meet there at noon.

She rang off and I called Pie to let him know what was up.

I pulled into the Fire Pit lot as Freddy was getting out of her car. We entered the restaurant and snagged a table in a back corner.

"OK," Freddy said. "Tell me about the Biology Center."

The waiter said, "The daily specials are wonderful...."

Freddy said, "We both want hamburgers medium rare."

"But the specials," the waiter said, "are..."

Freddy said, "Go get our hamburgers. And coffee."

"Would you like to see our wine list?"

Freddy said, "Go.Get.Our.Hamburgers.And. Coffee.Now."
The waiter scurried off.

Freddy could be a frightening woman.

Freddy and I met during the reign of the former LIT director. She's a stocky woman, fiftyish, her short, dark hair beginning to go gray. You might have taken her for a salesclerk in a downscale department store. She's easy to underestimate until such time as she lowers the boom. That happened to one of our former Center directors. He is no longer with LIT.

I launched into the narrative. "Calling it the 'Biology Center' is really not accurate. We only do plant biology and then only that segment of plant biology that's of use to industry. Which is not to say that our research is unimportant. It's very important. It helps feed the United States as well as the rest of the world."

Freddy gave me The Look. "Skip the commercials."

"Oh, alright. The Lab covers most aspects of plant biology. We don't do taxonomy which doesn't, at least as far as I know, serve industry's needs. What we look at is the structure of plants, how they grow and develop, and how they interact with their environment. The Lab is blessed with a great director, Molly Cameron."

The waiter arrived with our burgers and coffee, plunked them down before us, and fled.

"Tell me about Cameron," Freddy ordered. "Is she from the same mold as Alex?"

"She is," I said, "but not as cuddly. "She's interviewing now for a cell biologist to replace a retiree. Molly's been interviewing scientists for over a month; there's a long list of applicants.

Working under Molly Cameron is a plum job. Molly doesn't interfere with her staff. She hires excellent people and lets them do their thing. When they publish, they publish under their own names; she doesn't demand courtesy co-authorship. If one of the staff screws up, Molly takes the fall. And above all, she's a first-rate scientist."

Freddy asked, "How'd you get her?"

I grinned. "An historical imperative. The first Director of LIT was Rita Hicks, a terrifyingly competent woman. Do you know of her?"

Freddy shook her head.

I continued, "From what I understand, she wasn't much of a scientist, but she was a great manager, a student of Peter Drucker."

Freddy looked at her watch. I'll stipulate her credentials. Go on."

"Hicks was handed the two Centers and given the responsibility for staffing them. She recruited both Center directors. The CompSci Center went through a couple of directors before LIT lured Alex away from NASA a few years ago. In contrast, the BioCenter has remained stable. Hicks hired Molly, who had been a student of Barbara McClintock."

That caught Freddy's attention. "The Nobelist? From Carnegie's genetics lab in Cold Spring Harbor? Didn't she die a little while ago?"

I nodded. "Just last year. She outlived Hicks, who had died earlier of a very a fast-growing cancer. Anyhow, for the short time that Hicks was Director of LIT, the CompSci Center and the BioCenter received pretty even-handed treatment. As you have cause to know, the Director who replaced her wasn't in Hicks' league. He was interested in only two things: himself and computers. The BioCenter languished. Molly tried to wait the damnfool out, but she was on the verge of resigning when Pie took the helm. Under Pie, both Centers are flourishing."

"I take it," Freddy said, "that you're a fan and a friend of Cameron."

I started to laugh.

"Okay," Freddy said, "What?"

I told her about the retirement party.

"I don't understand," said Freddy, "how you lunatics manage to maintain one of the most productive units in the Federal government. Almost makes me believe in miracles."

Freddy finished her burger. "The Congressman wants to increase the BioCenter's funding. What are your thoughts?"

"Both Centers could use another bench scientist or two. Bio's greenhouse could use some expanding. But LIT has a remarkable chemistry going for it. Part of that is because Pie has been as even-handed as Hicks was – despite the fact that he's a biologist. If you unbalance the funding you're liable to set up resentments and destroy the chemistry."

Freddy laughed. "So you think we should throw money at *both* Centers."

"Well yes," I said, "of course."

Freddy laughed again. "You may be right." She waved at the waiter, who approached warily. She took the bill. "I'll buy. Wouldn't look good if you treated."

"You mean someone might think I bribed you with a

hamburger and coffee? You come cheap, lady."

We got into our respective cars and headed for our respective offices. I should explain about OMB. If you're a manager in a unit such as LIT or the Forensic Lab, there are several exterior government organizations that can gum up your works. LIT, for instance, sends its requested budget, with an explanation of what it'll spend the money on, to the Department. The Department sends it back with questions and "suggestions". That is, they tell us how they want it revised. There are several iterations of this exercise. It's not so bad now, with Pie at the helm, but it used to be hell under his predecessor. Pie has taken most of the heat off because of his eminence. Wouldn't look good if were to throw up his hands and walk off.

Anyway, once the budget is revised to DoTI's satisfaction, those guys combine it with the budgets of the other units in the Department and send the whole thing to the Office of Management and Budget – Freddy's bailiwick. And the whole thing gets done all over again. Then it is sent to Congress. It goes first to the Authorization Committee which says if it's okay to fund the various units. Once okayed, the budget is sent to the Appropriations Committee which approves the level of funding – which may or may not be what everyone or anyone asked for in the first place. At each step, there are multiple meetings by lots of people jumping through lots of hoops. All of these efforts to save the taxpayers' money cost quite a lot.

I picked up the bag of cookies, headed toward the BioCenter, and pushed open the double doors that lead into Molly's domain.

Because, in contrast to the Forensic Lab, DNA contamination is not a factor. Much of the work can be and is done on tables in a large open room. Offices are used for computer-and-paperwork. Office doors usually stay open. It's a friendly place – an atmosphere that pays off in productive interactions.

Another set of double doors, at the back of the open room, leads to a greenhouse. Compared to commercial and university greenhouses, the BioCenter's greenhouse is small – about four hundred square feet. Most of the space is devoted to benches that hold trays of experimental plants. As a rule, those plants have been created by LIT scientists together with industry scientists and sit in the controlled climate of the greenhouse to develop. The trays are not of much interest to the casual, non-biologist. But every once in a while, something gorgeous springs up – such as the ornamental hybrids – and then the computerniks from Alex's lab sneak over to take a peek. Molly puts up with them.

The extremely eminent and extremely pregnant Dr. Hodler looked up as I entered the BioCenter's space. She gave a welcoming shout, "Woo hoo, look who's here!"

Bench scientists looked up; heads popped out of office doors, all of them laughing. Except Molly, who marched up to me and demanded to know what was in the bag. Cookies.

She took a little bag, beckoned a young intern, and directed him to put the rest of the cookies in the lab kitchen. She then looked at me, saying "I hope you don't think this offering will save you from vengeful retaliation." She took her personal bag of cookies and marched back to her office.

I had rather been hoping that it *would* save me. Fooey!

A beat-up old Ford was awaiting our arrival on the road near the Bella Villa turnoff. Lomas and Arthur got out of the junker as the Mustang approached. In contrast to Lomas, who is a stocky, coffee-colored man of medium height, Arthur is a great, big, ebony, giant built along the lines of a brick outhouse. I introduced them to Alex and we decided that Lomas would ride with Alex in the Mustang and I would join Arthur in the junker. That way, if one of the cars took a wrong turn, both cars would still be able to arrive at the sheriff's office in good order. As a needless extra precaution, I explained that our route would turn down the Bella Villa road, pass Cabot House with its little patch of woods, and arrive in town.

Lomas asked, "What's Cabot House?"

Alex offered the description. "It's a combined Conference Center, restaurant, formal garden, wetland, and wedding venue. Neat place. It's a fixture in Bella Villa."

The ride to Bella Villa in the junker was interesting. The interior of the car was immaculate – not a mote of dust on the upholstery or the dashboard. Of more interest was the variety of rattles and bangs. Bass rumbles from somewhere in back. A crooner's whisper surrounding the front seat. A rather lovely descant from above. I was just getting into the rhythm when we arrived at Bella Villa. We pulled in behind the Mustang, which had just been parked near the sheriff's lot. Alex and Lomas went around back to check in with Sam and inspect Lomas's newly-purring wagon.

Arthur and I got out of the junker, Arthur bringing his practice board and sticks. He laid the board on the trunk to practice.

I was leaning against the fender when Petey arrived.

Petey is a twelve year old kid with the mental age of a six year old. No matter how old he gets, he will always, mentally, be six. He's the son of Claude and Midge Petrofsky. They own the hardware store; Claude is Bella Villa's mayor.

Petey's great adventure occurred about a year ago, when he fell asleep in the bed of Daryl Junior's pickup truck. Unnoticed, he was transported to Oxford, Maryland where he wandered around town for several days, sleeping in a boathouse and eating from the refrigerators of unlocked houses. All of Bella Villa was in an uproar as the townsfolk searched for Petey, until the kid finally decided he had seen enough of Oxford and let someone know that he wanted to go home.

Petey is a particularly nice boy. He is friendly, courteous – or as courteous as he can be given his six-year-old curiosity – and sunny. The whole town loves him. Matrons feed him cookies and milk. Geezers, whose own kids are grown and gone, take him fishing. And his parents adore him.

Petey took in the scene. He looked up at Arthur and asked, "Why is your skin black?"

Arthur looked down at Petey, "I dunno. Why is your skin white?"

"It's not," said Petey, "it's kind of pink."

Arthur regarded him seriously, "You're right."

"Why are you hitting that board?"

"I'm a musician," Arthur said. "I play the drums, but a drum is too big and too noisy to carry around, so I practice on this. Would you like to try?"

"Yes," said Petey, "but I don't think I can do it. I'm not very smart."

"Well, now," said Arthur, "there's all kinds of smart. There's smart that can figure things out. There's smart that can draw real nice pictures. And there's smart that can play music. Are you sure that you're not music smart?"

While this conversation was going on, Claude and Midge had walked up, unnoticed by either Arthur or Petey.

"No," said Petey. "How can I find out if I'm music smart?"

Arthur picked up the practice board and set in on a nearby bench. "Watch me." He tapped a rhythm. Bum bum bum bum bum. Bum bum bum bum bum. He handed the sticks to Petey and held the board steady. "Now you do it."

Petey held the sticks awkwardly and banged the board.

"Not bad," said Arthur. "Here, let me show you how to hold the sticks." He adjusted Petey's grip.

"Now, when I say 'bum', you hit the board real easy."

Petey followed instructions.

"Now, I'm going to say 'bum bum'. You follow." Petey followed, hitting the board twice, once with each hand, real easy.

By this time a small crowd had gathered.

"Okay, now let's try something harder" 'bum bum bum bum bum bum bum bum'".

Petey, delighted, managed the phrase.

"Well," Arthur said, "I think you just might be music smart. I tried to teach lots of kids that, and you the only one got it right the first time. You think your momma and daddy might get you some lessons?"

I looked over at Claude and Midge. Midge was trying not to cry.

Claude stepped up. "I'm Petey's dad. Claude Petrofsky." He held out his hand.

Arthur's gigantic paw swallowed it up. "Arthur Burbank. I wasn't just making him feel good. He really might have some talent. That rhythm is hard to get the first time. Won't know until you let him try.

"My wife runs a daycare center and she got a few retarded kids in it. One little girl showed a real artistic streak, so we took her to the National Gallery to see the pictures. When we came home she drew a picture that looked a lot like that Whistler painting, the Girl in White. I mean, like it wasn't Whistler, but for a ten year old retarded kid, it was the bomb. You never know with these kids. Anything's possible."

Claude considered. "Would you be willing to teach him?"

Arthur said, "It'd be an honor. My trio don't play on Tuesday, Wednesday, and Thursday. I get off work at three, so I could teach him those three days. I could bring some drums when I come up and if you decide you want Pete to continue, you can get him a set of his own."

Petey looked exultant.

Claude said, "How much would you charge?"

"Charge? Nothin', man. I'd like to do it."

Midge entered the conversation. "We can't let you do that. All that gas just getting up here and..."

Arthur cut in. "Let's do this then. When I come up, I'll leave the car at the Shell station and you can fill 'er up. I won't take any money for me, but my trio has a kind of Foundation. We collect money and buy instruments for the kids in the 'hood. You can make a donation. How's that suit?"

That suited just fine and the deal was struck.

Someone in the gathered crowd called out, "Way to go, Claude!" General applause.

Lomas, Sam, and Alex had arrived during the negotiations. They looked mightily pleased. Lomas tapped Arthur on the shoulder. "Lets bounce, dawg, we got rehearsal."

I was bemused as Lomas and Arthur drifted seamlessly between the King's English and ghetto slang.

The two musicians went to their respective vehicles, Lomas to the antique wagon in the sheriff's lot, Arthur to the junker on the street.

Claude and Midge started to walk away, but Sam stopped them.

Sam said, "Bea says that those two guys play in a terrific trio. How about we ask them to play after the Memorial Day parade?"

Claude thought. "Can they play, uh, real music?"

I answered, "They can play just about anything. Except hip hop. They don't do hip hop."

"We-ell," Claude scratched his chin. "I dunno. It would be a little unusual."

Midge entered the conversation. "Why not, Claude? It might be fun."

"We-e-ll," more chin scratching. "Where would they play? We don't have a bandstand. I've been pushing for a bandstand for years, but these cheapskates...."

"That's not a problem," Midge said. "We could borrow the little stage that the school uses for music events on the Green. It looks just like a mini-bandstand. Come on, Claude, they're being so nice to Petey, we should hire them for something."

Claude caved. "Alex, can you or Bea get in touch with them and have them call me? If they can do it, I'll make the arrangements over the phone."

"Our pleasure," Alex said.

Arriving home, we noticed an almost-new Taurus parked in front of the house. Alex drove up a few doors and pulled into a vacant space. We walked back to find Chrissie in conversation with our recently acquired next-door neighbor. They were looking at Marilyn's window box.

"Hey, Chrissie," Alex called.

The two women turned. "Oh, hi, Dr. Carfil. Mrs. Notte was about to go buy some pansies, but I've got something better in the trunk of the car. I was bringing them for your window box, but I've got enough for both. We hybridized them in the lab and we got more plants than we bargained for. If they work out, they'll bloom most of the summer. "

"Thanks, Chris. Is the trunk unlocked?"

Chrissie nodded.

Alex said, "Stay here. Bea and I will get them."

Alex and I walked down the steps to the Taurus. When we were out of earshot, Alex asked, "Why did Chrissie drive all the way here from the University? Couldn't she have just given them to you tomorrow at LIT?"

I laughed. "I think she wants to show off her new car."

"Oh," Alex said, "I can relate to that."

We each took a few plants back up the stairs. "Are these daylilies?" I asked.

"Yep," Chrissie said. "There've been continuous bloomers for about fifteen years, but we're trying to get more colors and to lengthen the bloom time. Even if they aren't as hardy as we think they'll be, or they don't survive in the window boxes, they'll at least be better than pansies."

"Why wouldn't they survive in a window box?" Alex asked.

"They'll be okay this year, at least," Chrissie said, "but they spread with rhizomes, and I'm not sure how they'll cope with the confined space. Like it or not, you're part of our experiment."

Johnny opened the door and exited his house. "Wassup?"

Marilyn introduced Johnny to Chrissie.

"You got more plants inna trunk?" he asked.

"We do," Alex said.

"Okay, le's get 'em."

"Wait a minute," Chrissie said. "Bring up the bag of manure, too."

Incredulous, Johnny asked, "You sayin' a bag a shit's inna car?"

"Johnny," Marilyn said, "watch your language."

"What watch? Dat's what it is."

Chrissie was laughing. "But it's a very special kind of shit. It's alpaca shit."

"Whassat?"

Now Alex and I were laughing.

Chrissie tried to explain between giggles. "It's a cute animal. It's related to a camel."

Johnny stared at her. "You mean like it spits?"

"Well, not usually at people."

"Not usually, huh. Well 'ats a comfort."

By this time, Alex and I were practically collapsed. I finally managed to stop laughing long enough to say, "We have some alpaca pictures inside. Why don't you guys get the rest of the plants while I get the pictures."

The men obediently scooted downstairs.

By the time I found the pictures, the flowers had been delivered and the planting had been started. Work stopped while I handed the photos around.

"Huh," Johnny said. "Dey *are* cute."

Alex and I tended to our window box while Chrissie helped Marilyn and Johnny with their planting and manure spreading.

Eventually, the urban farming complete, Chrissie departed.

"Nice kid," Johnny said.

Alex got the Mustang and returned it to its rightful slot.

We both took showers before sitting down to dinner. Alpacas are clean animals, but they're not all *that* clean.

CHAPTER 6
May 26, 1993

I stuck my head out of the window and admired my newly planted daylilies. I had never before seen a daylily-planted window box, but who's to say we weren't the forerunners of a nationwide trend? We had divided up the colors with the Nottes. They chose to go monochromatic. They had a gorgeous wine, with a greenish-yellow core, then a straight red, a curly red, and a magenta. Which pretty much covered that section of the spectrum. Our haul was more eclectic. It included a butterscotch, an apricot, a pale pink, and a spectacular white with wine trim. I looked over at the Notte's box and encountered Marilyn looking over at ours.

Marilyn called. "She's a really nice kid. Is she your niece or something?"

"Something. She's the daughter of a guy on my staff."

"I'da liked a kid like that but Johnny and I can't have any. You got kids?"

"No. Not a one."

Marilyn, bless her, didn't ask questions. Mafia or not, I think they'll be really good neighbors.

Alex called from within. "You want to split the last waffle?"

I waved at Marilyn and pulled my head in. "Don't mind if I do."

It was another top-down day. I loved it but the farmers must be getting worried.

Alex asked, "Do you remember when you got *your* first car?"

"Do I ever. It was an old Dodge that I bought off a used car lot for fifty bucks. It had a one month warrantee. On the thirty second day of my ownership, the engine dropped onto the pavement. Getting the engine plus the car towed to the junk yard cost more than the fifty bucks I paid for it."

Alex chuckled, "Alright, enough of this chitchat. You got a line that will satisfy the biologists?"

"I do. *A silly vegetarian felon,*"

"Come on," said Alex, "there's no such thing as a vegetarian felon. Vegetarians are upright citizens. Tree huggers."

"As a general rule, yes, but not my guy. That's why he's silly. So stop stalling and shoot me a line."

"Okay, you asked for it. *Swiped a bushel of peas and a melon,*"

"Oh boy. Hmmm." I pulled into the right lane, preparatory to getting off the freeway.

"Stumped, huh?" Alex gloated. "My turn to choose restaurants. And you know what the weather report says?"

"I shouldn't ask, but what?"

Alex grinned. "Chile today, hot tamale."

"Prior to our marriage, I wasn't aware that you had a cruel streak."

"Do you have the next lines or don't you?"

"Of course I do. *Then he sat down and ate, Off a Haviland plate*,"

Alex frowned. "What's a Haviland plate?"

"Haviland is a brand of fine china."

"Guys aren't supposed to know these things! That's not fair."

I snickered. "The rules don't say anything about fair. Does a last line occur to you?"

"You are a merciless woman. *Which he stole in the Straits of Magellan*. So there!"

I turned onto the road to LIT. The former Alligator Wrestling Emporium had now been painted a dark olive color. Windows had been cut and decorative deep wine colored shutters had been added. The same wine color graced the door, which was set off by black iron wall sconces.

"Wow!" Alex wowed. "I wonder what it's going to be."

"I doubt if it'll be another alligator wrestling place."

"No, it won't," Alex agreed. "Maybe a real upscale porn store."

"The only thing worse would be if they kept alligators in the back."

I drove past and up the road.

I pulled into the LIT lot and maneuvered the Mustang into the parking space. Our fans were milling about.

I got out of the car and clapped my hands. Instant silence and expectant demeanors.

"A silly vegetarian felon,

Swiped a bushel of peas and a melon,
Then he sat down and ate
Off a Haviland plate,
Which he stole in the Straits of Magellan"

The huddle didn't last long. Raspberries.

Disconsolate, Alex shuffled off to the CompSci Lab. Equally morose, I headed toward the admin wing. Don caught up with me. "Don't feel bad. It was a good try."

I mustered a sinister smile. "You'd better tell those people to treat us with more respect. We're connected."

"What's that supposed to mean?"

"I'll tell you when we get to Pie's office. How's the remodeling going?"

"Bunch of morons," Don growled.

"What now?"

"We're not just remodeling the house, we're remodeling that little mother-in-law cottage out back. We're enlarging it so it'll have two bedrooms instead of one and adding a garage."

"Why are you doing that?"

"When the kids come home at breaks, they'll have a a little privacy. Connie's ancient aunt died and left her some money so we can afford to do it. Anyway, the contractor measured for the garage and built a two-floor addition with the new bedroom on the second floor and the garage below. He got the measurement wrong and the garage is too narrow."

"You can't get the car in?" I asked.

"Oh, the car will get in, alright. You just can't get out of the car. Morons."

"What are you going to do?"

"The contractor will have to remove the outside wall on both stories and build out. He's balking but he's going to have to do it."

I started to laugh.

Don looked at me suspiciously, "What's funny?"

"Maybe if the car had a sunroof, the contractor could cut a hole in the floor above and have one of those attic pull-down ladders and..."

"Ha ha," Don said. He didn't look amused.

"How about this? Only build out the ground floor, reinforce the roof, add a door to the second floor bedroom, and make a little porch there. Would that be easier to do?"

Don thought. "It might. Thanks."

Lenore was at her guard desk as we walked up. She said, "Marge brought two small coffee cakes in. Do you want me to bring one and some coffee to Pie's office?"

Don answered affirmatively and we continued on.

Pie was looking a bit off of his normally unruffled self.

"What's wrong, Pie?" I asked.

He said. "You know that *momser* who was blackmailing people?"

I nodded.

"Tokke? He was found shot in the back of the head. It looks like a mob killing."

A vision of that nice Johnny Notte flashed through my mind. Oh dear.

Pie went on. "Paul Richards asked if you could continue at the Forensic Lab for a few more days."

"For heaven's sake, why?"

"He said that they expect that *meshuggener* congressman to come around and they think it would be a good idea if someone besides Lab personnel observed his behavior."

"That's ridiculous."

Pie laughed. "I know. I think he wants a shoulder to cry on. But if you're not too busy here, it would be okay with me."

I looked at Don. "Will you need me for anything?"

Don said, "Nothing I can think of. If something comes up, we can always call you. But before Pie gave us the News of the Week, you were saying that you were connected. Who you connected to?"

Lenore came in with coffee cake and beverage. She stuck around to help us nibble and to listen to my reply.

"'Connected' is a term we Wise Guys use to signify that we have ties to the Mafia."

Lenore looked shocked. "You have ties to the *Mafia*?"

Don asked, "Since when?"

Pie just shook his head.

"Since yesterday," I said. "A Mafia guy and his wife moved in next door. She and Chrissie and I went gardening together."

Lenore said, "You *really* have ties to the Mafia?"

Pie laughed. "Find out if they can get you something better than that clunker you're driving."

Lenore began to edge toward the door.

111

We finished the coffeecake and Lenore seized the moment to depart with the crumbs.

"So *nu*," inquired Pie, "what should I tell Richards? Do you want to go back to Forensic for a few days?"

I thought about it. "Okay. I must admit I'm curious about how this Brattice thing comes out. But I can't start until tomorrow. I need today to clear up the junk in my in-box."

I passed Lenore's desk on my way to clearing up the junk. She eyed me warily.

Ben was seated in my office, waiting for me. He was grinning. "So Johnny's your new neighbor, huh?"

I sat down. "That he is. He's an improvement on the old neighbor."

"I stopped for a drink on the way home, last night. Johnny was there. He said if I saw you before he did, I should tell you that it wasn't a mob hit. He thinks someone went into business for himself. He said you'd explain. So explain, please."

"You know that guy you and Chuck said was into the mob for a gambling debt?"

Ben nodded.

"He turned up dead from a bullet to the back of his head. Looks like a mob killing but now that I think about it, that doesn't make sense. You can't collect a gambling debt from a corpse."

"True." Ben pondered. "So someone has committed a grave offense."

Ben departed.

As I was driving home, Alex was thinking. Finally, he said, "If it wasn't a mob killing, then whodunit?"

I shrugged. "I only know a small part of the Forensic Lab and even that limited field has a gaggle of candidates. Jazz is still hurting from the incarceration years, when Cody's family very nearly pauperized her grandfather. Giles must be terrified that Cody will reveal his Black ancestor. Danielson has reason to hate him for destroying her niece. And God knows who else would like to see him dead."

"Yeah," Alex remarked, "but there's something out of kilter there."

"Oh?"

"Why now?" Alex said. "The motives you just listed have been there for some time. So why knock him off now?"

"Good point. I suppose Cody may have upped the ante on Elliott Giles, but I can't think of anything that might have sent either Jazz or Danielson into a murder mode just now. It bears thinking about."

Alex and I were finishing up the last of our dinner when the doorbell rang. We got up, noticing the flashing blue light shining through our window. We opened the door. Sam was standing there. He said, "Chrissie was raped."

I said, "No. No. That didn't happen."

Alex put his arms around me.

"I'm afraid it did, Bea. She's in the little hospital in Bella Villa. She asked for you. But there's a major accident on the

Beltway. No way for you to get there quickly. So I brought a squad car to cut through the mess. Walt's in the car. He'll lead the way. I'll ride with you and explain what happened. That'll save time."

Alex and I left the house immediately, pausing only to pick up the car keys.

Johnny had noticed the blue flashers and came out of his door. He called, "Whass goin' on?"

Alex called back, "Chrissie was raped. We're going to be with her."

Johnny was thunderstruck. "Dat sweet kid? Oh, Jesus!"

He called to Marilyn, who was about to join him. "Go back in, Merry, it ain't for us."

We got in the Mustang, Alex in the driver's seat. Both Sam and I got in back. We pushed the passenger seat as far forward as it would go, to make it easier for Alex to hear the explanation.

Walt gave a warning squeal of the squad car siren and we took off.

Sam said, "Joe and I were on foot patrol near that little grove of trees near Cabot House. We heard a scream and we ran into the trees. Chrissie was there, with a guy on top of her. He jumped up and started running. Joe chased him.

"I went to Chrissie. She was whimpering. When I bent down she said, 'No. Please don't.' I didn't know what to do. I couldn't leave her there. So finally I told her that it was okay and I picked her up. She kept saying, 'Please don't.' But I had to get her to the hospital. I carried her to the squad car and got her into the passenger's seat. By the time we got to the hospital, Chrissie was not only whimpering but shaking. Finally she asked if you would come to her. I told her you would. I stayed in the waiting room while they examined her. They took her clothes for evidence of rape, gave her a hospital gown, and brought her into a private room. Once she was settled, I got Walt and we came to get you. You wouldn't have been able to get there for at least four hours. If then."

Alex asked, "Did Joe catch the bastard?"

"Don't know. I left before he got back."

Walt led us to the Beltway, which was a mess. A trailer truck was on its side. Cars were strewn across all lanes. Traffic was at a halt while ambulances, tow trucks, and state troopers did their respective things. We moved onto the paved shoulder. Walt turned on the siren and we took off, fast, weaving our way around debris. We finally cleared the last of the wreckage and *really* took off.

We reached the hospital and the three of us got out of the car. Walt ran up. "Gimme the keys, I'll park the car and return them." Alex surrendered the keys and we went through the hospital doors. Sam led us to the waiting room. It's a small room, as befits a small hospital. A few faded prints hang on the standard institutional green walls. About a dozen plastic-cushioned chairs are randomly arranged. No one was seated on any of them. There is a Reception desk but no one was behind it. Jim and Jeanne were standing near the desk, both of them crying. A pudgy, officious looking man stood in front of them with his arms folded.

Alex asked, "Where's Chrissie?"

"No one," said Pudge, "is allowed to speak with her until after the rape counselor talks to her."

"So when will the rape counselor be finished talking to her?"Alex asked.

"We've sent for her. She's not here yet."

Alex and I looked at one another. We just came all the way from Alexandria and the rape counselor wasn't here yet?

Sam said, "She must be tied up in the accident traffic."

I addressed Pudge. "Are you telling us that Chrissie is alone in a room with no one to comfort her?"

"Those are the rules," he said. "Only family can see her."

I looked at Jim. He said, "Chrissie doesn't want me there. She doesn't want any man there. Not even me. And this guy won't let Jeanne in to help her because we aren't married yet." Tears were coursing down his cheeks.

Pie and Bessie had arrived in time to hear both exchanges. Pie said, "We would have come earlier, but we were out to dinner. We found Sam's message on the answering machine when we got home. We came here right away, with a stop at the cabin to get clothes for Chrissie. Who's that *shmegegge?*" He pointed to Pudge.

"The hospital administrator," Sam said.

Bessie walked up to Pudge and announced, "I am Doctor Lee. Where is the patient?"

Pudge unfolded his arms. "Thank heavens you're here. These people are impossible."

He pointed to a corridor. "She's in that room closest to us. You can see it from here. Room 100."

Bessie entered the room. In just a few minutes she emerged. "Dr. Goode," she said, "would you come in, please?"

Bessie addressed Pudge, "We won't need you further." The *shmegegge* departed.

Bessie left the room as I entered.

Chrissie was in a hospital gown, huddled on the bed, her arms around her knees. I sat next to her. She started to cry.

"Dr. Goode, he. He. He." Sobs took over.

"You don't have to explain, Chrissie. Don't say anything until you want to."

We sat for several minutes. Then Chrissie said, "He just jumped out and knocked me down before I could do anything. I was walking back to my car from Jeanne's. We had dinner. Please don't go away."

"I'll stay as long as you need me."

Chrissie didn't say anything. Nor was she crying. She just let me hold her.

Eventually, the door opened and Miriam Manley, Ralph's wife, entered. She is a remarkably beautiful woman in her fifties. She exudes an aura of calm strength. She approached Chrissie. "Chrissie, I have to talk to you. You don't have to say anything, but you do have to listen to me."

Chrissie looked at me. "Dr. Goode..."

"I'll move right there," pointing to a chair, "where you can see me. Please listen to Mrs. Manley."

Chrissie nodded. Miriam sat on the bed next to her. "Give me your hand, Chrissie."

Chrissie offered her hand.

Miriam said, in that lovely Caribbean lilt of hers, "When I

was just a few years younger than you, in Trinidad, I was raped."

Chrissie started. "*You* were raped?"

Miriam smiled. "It happens. Trinidad is much different than here. At least I hope so. In Trinidad when a mature girl or a woman is raped, it is assumed that she asked for it. She is shamed. So of course, rape is seldom reported.

"I was a very popular mature girl. All of the football stars courted me. I had no time for anyone else. Then I was gang raped. I don't know who did it. I suppose I should have recognized them but it was a blur. After it was over I walked home. I told my parents what happened. My mother stayed in the living room with me. My father walked out of the room. He didn't look at me.

"Mama took me into the bathroom and cleaned me up. She sat with me all night in my bedroom but she didn't say anything. She didn't hold me. She just sat. In the early morning we went back to the living room. Someone knocked at the door. It was one of the boys that I never had time for. He was carrying a single flower. Mama told him to go away. He handed her the flower and she closed the door. She gave me the flower. After a while she peeked out the window. The boy was sitting on the steps. Mama shrugged. The boy sat on the steps until the school day started at ten o'clock.

"The next day, the same thing happened. The boy knocked on the door, produced a flower, Mama told him to go away, and he sat on the steps. This went on for four days. The fourth day was Saturday. No school. So he sat there all day.

"On the fifth day, when he knocked on the door, I asked Mama to let him in. She was reluctant, but finally she allowed him entry.

"He did not come close to me, but he told me that he loved me. That he had loved me since we were freshmen. And that he would do anything I wanted him to do. He would stay with me or he would go away. So I told him that I could not go outside. I could not see all of those people who thought I asked for it. But I would like him to bring me my homework assignments. It was so close to graduation time and I wanted to graduate.

"So he did that and we began to do our homework together. Then he brought me my diploma. And in all this time, my father did not appear.

"Then one day the boy came and he told me that he had been awarded a scholarship to the University of Michigan in the United States. He said that he would stay in Trinidad if I wanted him to or I could go to Michigan with him. His family had money. They would pay for me to go.

"Mama left the room and told my father. On hearing this, my father told Mama to tell me to go. So I went. I have not seen my parents again.

"It gets very cold in Michigan -- but even so, it is a good place, and Ralph and I got married." Miriam smiled. "That made it warmer, you see."

Chrissie laughed. "But you have children. How did....?"

Now Miriam laughed. "They were not immaculate conceptions. And that was the other thing I wanted to tell you. You don't think so now, but later, when you meet a man you love and he loves you, you will learn that sex with love is a beautiful thing. Not at all like what happened to you. What happened to you is horrible and it will stay with you for a while but the memory will fade.

"I will tell you how it was for me. For a long time I would go to bed and I would wake up screaming. I would relive that rape in every particular. Then after some months, I would wake but not screaming. I would remember that rape. But I would not relive it. There is a large difference between reliving and remembering. Then after some years, I would wake up only once in a while. And now I don't wake up at all."

"But," Chrissie said, "you have two large boys. Do they know?"

"Of course they know, they are our sons."

"But what do they think?"

Miriam laughed again. "They think that they must treat women with respect and that they must take very good care of their mother. I encourage that."

Chrissie burst out laughing.

"Well," Miriam said, "that is what I wanted to tell you. That and if you ever want to talk with me, I'm here for you."

Chrissie thought. "I have you, and Dr. Goode, and Dr. Lee, and Daddy and Jeanne. You had Dr. Manley. How does anyone get through this if they don't have someone they love and who loves them?"

Miriam shrugged. "I guess they call a crisis hotline."

Chrissie shook her head. "I couldn't talk to a stranger."

Miriam said, "You could if there were no one else. Now I'll give you back to Dr. Goode."

She got up. Chrissie said, "Would you tell Daddy that I'd like him to take me home now?"

Miriam nodded and left. Chrissie said to me, "Did you know?"

I shook my head.

Jim and Jeanne came in the room. Jeanne was carrying Chrissie's change of clothes.

Chrissie jumped off the bed and flung herself into Jim's arms. I left the room.

Pie, Bessie, Alex and Sam were still in the waiting room. As I approached them, Joe arrived. His face and a good bit of his uniform were caked with dried blood. Sam asked, "Did you catch him?"

"Yeah," Joe said, "He's in lockup."

Sam inspected him. "You've got blood all over you."

"Not my blood. He resisted arrest. I had to subdue him." He ran his fingers through his hair. I noticed that his knuckles were bruised .

Sam asked, "Did you ID him?"

Joe's mouth was a straight line. "Oh, yeah. By the time I got him locked up he was crying and saying he was gonna tell his papa on me."

"So who is he?"

"He's the son of an effing redneck Congressman. Jimboy Davies."

Chrissie, in fresh clothes, came into the waiting room with Jeanne and Jim. They walked toward the exit. Chrissie stopped in front of Sam. "Thank you, Sam," she said.

"You're welcome," said Sam.

The *shmegegge* reappeared. "Wait," he said, "you have to be discharged."

Sam said, "No she doesn't."

As they left, a stout woman entered. "I am Dr. Schiele. Where is my patient?"

CHAPTER 7
May 27, 1993

Alex and I woke up late, having spent the night crying, making tender love, and fitfully sleeping. We ate a mournful breakfast, cleaned up the dishes, and agreed that we were not up to a limerick. We drove, mostly in silence, to LIT, noticing neither the beautiful day nor the splendid display of roadside flowers. Alex pulled off the road once for a comfort snoggle.

We parked at LIT. About twenty scientists, mostly botanists, were waiting for us. As we got out of the car, a young man approached. He was a nice looking kid in a dark blue polo shirt and chinos. A couple of inches under six feet. About 150 pounds. Unruly shock of brown hair. Fit but not a body-builder. I recognized him as one of Molly's interns. Clearly, he had been crying.

"Dr. Goode," he said, "I'm Blake Halonen. We wondered if we could ask you something." He stifled a sob.

"Of course, Blake. What is it?"

"Well, Chrissie's going to come back to the lab, at least we hope so." He stopped to compose himself.

Alex put a hand on the kid's shoulder. "It's okay to cry, Blake. I've been doing it off and on since we found out what happened."

Blake swallowed. "Thanks, Dr. Carfill. This was just so awful. You know, it would be bad if it happened to anyone, but for it to be Chrissie...." He tailed off and started up again.

"Anyway, what we wondered was how do we treat her when she comes back. At least half of us are guys and we don't want to ... you know."

I looked at the kid. Tears were flowing freely down his cheeks. Miriam's narrative pushed itself to the top of my consciousness.

"Blake, are you in love with Chrissie?" Oh boy, was that insensitive! Too late to take it back.

"No, of course not. Well, I don't know. Well. Yes. I am."

I plowed on. "I've never been raped, so I don't really know if I'm telling you the right thing. But my gut feeling is that you should behave normally, don't offer sympathy but be gentle, and realize that Chrissie may act a bit erratically for a while. Put up with it.

"As for you, if you love her..."

"I do!"

"...then tell her. Don't come on strong, don't ask her to respond, but tell her."

"Dr. Goode, I don't know if I can do that. I mean, I have to get used to the idea myself."

"Then tell her when you get used to it."

The kid grinned through his tears. "That may be about half an hour from now. Thanks for the help."

He went back to the group.

My in-box held the news that a team from the Office of Management and Budget was going to appear the second week in June for the annual briefing. Unless something has happened since Freddy and I had lunch, she will be one of the analysts. And since we've established a good rapport with OMB, and since both Centers are ticking along pretty well, there shouldn't be a problem, even if Freddy is not one of the analysts. Only possible question might be why the hell I was spending all that time at the Forensic Lab. Perhaps my slot at LIT was superfluous. Hmmm. Maybe we just shouldn't mention the Forensic Lab.

I called Molly to let her know of the impending grill session. "I think OMB might be interested in plant breeding. They like to hear the word 'industry' and the plant breeding program has an obvious link."

Molly snorted. "Even to the bean counters at OMB?"

"I didn't know you were breeding beans. But yeah, the OMB analysts aren't dumb, just narrow. If I remember correctly, you said that it looks like your work will cause a significant increase in speed from lab to marketplace for a number of critical cultivars."

"Good God," Molly said, "you were actually listening."

"Sometimes I do. Anyway, if we're lucky, they'll send Freddy Langsteth, who may even be helpful. She's an astute woman. Does someone on the plant breeding team talk anything but biospeak?"

"Hodler can do it," Molly said. "if she's not introducing a baby. But you're right. That would be a good program to showcase. I can do the briefing if Hodler isn't available."

Well now. What if Hodler goes into labor in the middle of the briefing? OMB might never recover. Maybe we should ask her to keep her legs crossed until the session is over.

I said, "Outstanding! I'll give you more information as soon as I get it."

"Uh, Bea. Thanks for being nice to Blake. He's a great kid and I'm no good at the sympathy thing. He's really broken up about Chrissie; I didn't know how to make him feel better."

"I wasn't sure I was any help. Thanks for telling me."

"Do you think Chrissie will come back to the lab any time soon?"

I thought about it. "I don't know. She's had a traumatic experience. Some women never get over it. No woman gets over it right away, but some women can function almost normally pretty quickly, despite the turmoil that's still going on inside.

"I'd bet that Chrissie will be back sooner rather than later. Apart from Chrissie being Chrissie, your lab is a good place to come back to. In fact, that's true of all of LIT. There aren't the tensions that permeate a lot of other places."

Molly grunted. "Hate to admit it, but Pie, you, and Don have made the difference. And if you tell anyone I said that, I'll deny it!"

We rang off.

I started to Pie's office, but Lenore informed me that he was at a Departmental meeting and wouldn't be back until later in the afternoon. Also missing were Jim and Jeanne. They were staying with Chrissie at Jim's house.

I debated whether to call Jim to see how Chrissie was doing. On one hand, I didn't want to intrude. On the other hand, I wanted to see if there was anything I could do. I called.

Jeanne answered. Chrissie was better than expected. Was having some crying spells, but for the most part, she was acting as if nothing happened. She was insisting on going back to work tomorrow. Jeanne thought that the apparent calm might be the result of shock.

I agreed. "Are you going to let her come back to work?"

Jeanne said, "I don't see how we're going to stop her without making things worse."

And with that, we hung up.

My little group was now seriously depleted. I asked Marge and Lenore to join me in my office. Lenore offered to take the incoming phone calls for the whole group, which would free Marge to do everything else. Ben would lend some consulting advice should something require his area of expertise. The two women agreed to call me at the Forensic Lab if they got overwhelmed.

Marge said, "Do you know what some a-hole said to me a couple of years ago?"

"What?" Lenore asked .

"He said, 'What's the big deal about rape? It only means that the woman had sex when she didn't want to.'"

Lenore and I stared at her, aghast.

"What did you respond?" I asked.

"I smacked his face as hard as I could and said, 'That only means that you got a love pat when you didn't want one.' I guess I hit him a little harder than I thought. When I saw him a couple of days later he had a black eye."

I cajoled the clunker into taking me to the Forensic Lab, where I found Paul in solemn conversation with Jazz. Paul had found out Tuesday night that Cody was dead. The mail carrier had noticed that Cody's mail had not been picked up from his rural box for several days. So he walked up to the house to see if anything was wrong. He found the front door wide open and walked in. Cody was face down on the floor, the back of his head a mess. Once the postman got over the shock, he used Cody's phone to call 911. Then, bless him, he called the animal shelter, told them what happened, and asked them to get the dog who was barking in the yard.

Whatever else Cody's murder would cause, Team 3 was now seriously shorthanded. They were already down one analyst and now they were also down a supervisor. Paul had called Jazz, who agreed to come in that night to start picking up the slack. Scheduling the tasks to be done, she decided to move the material associated with the "closed" Brattice case from the active refrigerator to the archives, which were located in a room of their own. That room could only be entered with the use of the security card, and once inside, an additional security precaution required the use of a key to open the door of the "cage" where the archives were kept.

Ordinarily one of the techies would make the move, but they would have their hands full the next day. Jazz decided to do it herself. And immediately noticed that there was something funny about Adam Brattice's vial. The handwriting on the label, which should have been hers, wasn't. She checked the contents of the vial. It was plain water. She retrieved one of Adam's bone fragments from the archive and re-did the test. Adam's blue dots did not match Brat's. Just to make sure, Jazz tried another test – "Polymarker". There were even more differences between Adam's and the kid's DNA. Adam was not the father. This was one helluva mess.

"I think," Jazz said, "that I'd better check everything he did."

Paul pulled his goatee and nodded.

Jazz left.

Paul was clearly in a state. His hair was standing up. His mustache was askew. And his goatee was crying for mercy.

"This is unprecedented," he said. "I don't know what we can do beyond what we're doing. I can just pray that the Lab doesn't lose its accreditation. And I can pray harder that I don't lose my job."

I asked Paul if it was usual for a supervisor, such as Cody, to be involved in the "wet lab".

"I thought the analysts and technicians did the hands-on stuff?"

"That's the way it normally works, but we're short-handed, so Cody pitched in. He was good about that. We'll miss him."

"Yeah, right," I said. "A real selfless guy. Do you know if any reagents have gone missing this week?"

Paul looked startled. "I didn't think of that. I'll call Jazz and have her check."

"Paul, why don't we go check?"

Paul started to protest and then got my point; not probable, but Jazz could be the culprit. He said, "Let's go."

We walked to the PCR set-up room. Paul ushered me into the vestibule and said, "Wait here. I'll get you a lab coat and gloves. We wouldn't normally let an alien into the lab, but under the circumstances, I'd like you to do the counting. It's unlikely that I'd sabotage my own Lab, but just in case a question is raised, it would be better if an outsider did the checking. Before you leave, let's get a DNA sample from you just for a contaminant check."

I waited for Paul while he got the coat and gloves. We got ourselves outfitted, donned protective glasses, and entered the room. Two tall refrigerators and one small freezer stood against the back wall. Paul explained. "One of the fridges contains extracted material from the evidence. The second contains the DQ kits minus the polymerase enzymes, which are in the freezer. Since those are what's being stolen, those are what you need to count."

"Paul," I protested, "that freezer is set at -20 Celsius. I'll freeze!"

Paul laughed. "No you won't. They are all in vials and all of the vials are in one box. Just reach in and.... On second thought, to relieve your anxiety, *I'll* reach in and get the box, set the box on that table over there, and you unseal the box and count. This was a supplementary delivery, so the box hasn't been opened yet. It was going to be opened tomorrow when we're expecting new evidence.

"On the front of the box there will be a label that contains, among other information, the number of vials in the box. So get out of the way and I'll get the box."

I dutifully moved my *tuchas*.

Paul retrieved the box, set it on the table, and handed me a sharp tool for opening it. I looked at the label. "Fifteen." As expected. The box was sealed but there was no way of knowing if it had been unsealed and a substitute seal affixed.

I unsealed the box and counted the vials. "Fifteen there are. Keep counting for a week or two. If there are no more disappearances, that'll be pretty good indication that Cody was the thief."

Paul nodded sadly. We walked back to his office.

"By the way, do you know what will happen to Cody's dog?" I asked.

"Nothing good. Cody didn't have any family. Parents died a long time ago and he didn't have siblings. The dog had a tag with Cody's office phone number on it, so the shelter called the number and when Cody didn't answer, the call was forwarded to the Lab's secretary. I think you've met Bridget."

I nodded.

"Bridget let me know about the phone call and I checked with the staff here. Everyone who wanted a dog already has one, and no one else wants a pet. Particularly a great, big, galumpy puppy. So he's still at the shelter, but he'll be put down if he can't be placed."

"That's a shame. Cody loved the beast so there must be something lovable about him."

Paul's eyes lit up. "Do you want him?"

I laughed. "No, thank you. My alpacas would never forgive me."

Paul looked at me strangely but didn't say anything.

I asked, "Could you ask the shelter to postpone the execution until after the weekend? I may know someone who would give him a good home."

"Sure." He ran his fingers through his mustache. "I'd like your advice about something, Bea. What would you think about promoting Jazz to Supervisor?"

"I've only talked with her a couple of times and I have no way of judging her competence. But she is certainly well-spoken and congenial. From that meager base, I can't see any reason not to promote her. No warning bells have gone off."

"Good. Good. Now how about elevating either Giles or Danielson to the analyst slot?"

I kept my mouth shut.

Paul mussed his hair, which now looked as if it were about to take flight. "Warning bells?"

"You know I can't get seriously involved in your personnel decisions, Paul. But you also know that Danielson didn't report Cody's extracurricular ventures in blackmail."

Paul grunted. "And Giles?"

"No comment."

"Shit! Pardon my French. I was afraid your opinion would be the same as mine. I'll have to raid one of the teams that has two analysts. Thanks for the help."

I laughed. "I didn't say a word."

Paul's phone rang. "This is Richards." He listened. Hung up.

"Something's come up at LIT, Bea. They want you back there ASAP."

Now what? I told Paul I'd see him on the morrow and accompanied the clunker back to LIT.

Lenore looked grim as she waved me into Pie's office. The office was filled with Pie, Don, and Sam. None of them looked happy.

"Sit down, Bea."

I sat. "What's wrong?"

Pie said, "The *putz* got off."

"What? No way."

Don looked at the sheriff. "Play it again, Sam."

Sam nodded. "The whole thing stinks. His father visited him while the scumbag was in our jail. About an hour after his father left, we got a call that sonny boy had waived a jury trial and the judge had moved the proceedings up. He was going to hear the case as soon as we could get to the courthouse. We drove the scumbag up to the courthouse and took him in. His father was in the courtroom; the judge was already on the bench. Joe and I told him what happened. Then the scumbag testified that the sex had been consensual.

"The judge asked him how he had met Chrissie, or 'that woman' as he called her.

"Scumbag said that he and his father had stopped at The

133

Rabbit Hole after an inspection trip to the Forensic Lab. Chrissie had been there having dinner with Jeanne. When Jeanne went to the restroom, Chrissie came on to him. They agreed to meet in the woods near Cabot House. Jimboy Senior confirmed that scenario."

"Get out! That's a pure fabrication."

"That it is," said Sam. "Then the judge asked him why he ran away. 'Oh,' said the scumbag, 'there were these great big men running into the woods and I got scared.' He was just so ashamed of himself. He should have stayed to protect the girl. But he just didn't think. The adrenaline simply kicked in and he ran."

I put my head in my hands.

"The judge then asked if 'the woman' was in the courtroom. He knew damn well she wasn't. Even if we'd known it was a set-up, he didn't leave time for us to get Chrissie and Jeanne to the Courthouse to testify. So he said that in the absence of evidence to the contrary he could not ruin the life of 'this fine young man' and pronounced him not guilty."

I was incredulous. "Just like that?"

"Just like that," said Sam. "Scumbag went to join his father and actually smirked at Joe on the way out. I had to hold Joe back. I think he would have killed that scumbag if I hadn't grabbed him. Joe's got three girls of his own and I think he envisioned each one of them under the scumbag. If he ever gets his hands on that... *putz?*" He looked at Pie.

"*Putz,*" Pie agreed.

"...he really will kill him."

"So Jimboy paid off the judge," I said.

"Can you think of another explanation?" Don asked.

I shook my head.

As Alex backed the Mustang out of its parking place I told him about the courtroom fiasco.

"Oh, no! So that bucket of slime is free to rape again."

"That seems to be the case," I acknowledged. "Joe took it pretty hard."

"I wonder how the scumbag knew Chrissie would be in the woods."

"Not a big mystery," I said. "I think he did see Chrissie in The Rabbit Hole and just stalked her until she obligingly led him to a good place for rape. She had walked Jeanne home and then started back to get her car. It was parked near Cabot House. She and Jeanne had probably been looking at the gardens before they walked to The Rabbit Hole."

We drove in silence until we approached the Bella Villa turnoff.

Alex said, "I think this is a day when Arthur's coaching Petey. Do you want to check in with them? I feel a need to associate with decent people."

"Good thought. Let's go."

We pulled up near Chuck's museum and found all three members of the trio, along with their instruments, there. The school's little bandstand had been placed between them and the museum. It looked quite at home there.

We got out of the car and demanded an explanation of their

presence. They laughed. Lomas said, "We're playing here Memorial Day and wanted to scope out the venue."

"How's Petey coming along?" Alex asked.

"Comin' good," Arthur answered. "I think we may have a Max Roach on our hands."

Alex chuckled. "I'll settle for an Arthur Burbank."

Willis asked, "How's Chrissie doin'? I hope that guy gets the chair."

Alex and I looked at one another.

Lomas asked, "What's wrong?"

Alex told them.

Lomas said, "He walked?"

I replied, "He walked."

Lomas said, quietly, "I'll kill the motherfucker."

Willis said, "Wrong, bro. *We'll* kill the motherfucker."

Arthur said, "You got *that* right."

I looked at Lomas. He looked thunderous. I looked at Willis. He looked dangerous. I looked at Arthur. He looked murderous.

Just then, Petey walked up. "Hello, Dr. Goode. I saw your car. Did you come to watch me?"

I looked again at the trio. The three thugs had disappeared and the amiable *We Three* had returned.

Arthur grinned at Petey. "Naw. No one can watch us practice, not even Dr. Goode and Dr. Carfil. You'll have an audience when you get a little better."

"When will that be, Mr. Burbank?"

"Just a few more days, Petey."

"Oh. That's alright then."

Petey ambled off.

Alex said, "Don't you guys do anything stupid. You can't take care of Petey if you're playing pinochle in the penitentiary."

Lomas, the high school music teacher, responded. "Of course not, Alex. We were just mouthing off. We wouldn't dream of doing anything violent."

I glanced at Arthur and Willis. They were solemnly nodding agreement. They undoubtedly had their fingers crossed behind their backs.

We continued the voyage home.

Alex asked, "Do you think they'll, uh, off him?"

"Either they will or Joe will."

Alex pondered. "Between the trio and Joe, I wouldn't bet a plugged nickel on the scumbag living another month."

Johnny was getting out of his car at the same time that we dismounted the Mustang. "How's Chrissie doin'?"

We filled him in.

"You tellin' me da *schmuck* is loose?"

"That's what we're telling you," Alex said.

"Excuse me," Johnny said politely as he moved toward his door. "I gotta make a phone call."

Alex and I looked at one another.

I said, "Among Joe, the trio, and Johnny, I wouldn't bet a brass button on the scumbag living another *week*."

CHAPTER 8

May 28, 1993

I caught a quick glimpse of myself in the bathroom mirror as I got out of the shower. I looked closer as I toweled off. My shortish auburn hair wasn't looking so auburn. Gray strands were intruding. I thought about this while I dressed. Alex was watching me think.

"What?" he asked.

"Do you think I should cut my hair shorter?"

Alex climbed into his trousers. "If you cut your hair any shorter you'll look like Sinead O'Connor. Do you want to look like Sinead O'Connor?'

"Nothing against Sinead O'Connor, but no."

"God is merciful," Alex said. "Lox and bagels today?"

"Lovely." I got two bagels out of the freezer and popped them in the oven to warm up enough to slice and toast. While I was doing that, Alex retrieved the lox and unwrapped the cream cheese.

"Ratchenfrachit!" he growled.

"What's wrong?"

"The cream cheese is moldy. Do you think we can cut the mold out?"

He looked hopefully at me. I glared at him.

"No," he said, "I guess not. Start the coffee. I'll walk over to the grocery store and get more cheese. By the way, do you remember where we put our exercise shorts?"

"I think they're in the trunk in the basement. Right next to my exercycle and your rowing machine. Why?"

"Weather report says it might get to ninety today. I think we should bring some serious summer clothes."

"I'll take a quick look in the basement while you're at the store," I promised.

Alex left and I went out to the patio. Our planters were in serious need of replenishment. Given the lack of rain and our neglect of watering, it was no wonder. Maybe Chrissie could produce some more goodies from the BioCenter. Which reminded me of Chrissie. I sat down on one of the planters, fighting tears. I couldn't love that kid more if she were my own.

I'm not an introspective person. For the most part, when things happen I just take note and go about my business. Unless it's something I can fix. At which time I fix it and *then* go about my business. But sometimes a cataclysm occurs, such as when Harry and my unborn kid were killed. Then I probably introspect too much. Which is what I was doing while sitting on the planter.

Why did I love Chrissie so deeply? Was she just a surrogate for the kid I didn't and couldn't ever have? I didn't think so. Alex and I had discussed adoption and decided against it. We didn't *need* a kid. But what I felt for Chrissie wasn't need. It was undiluted love. And there was no way that I could "fix" Chrissie and then go about my business. But ever since the time when Chrissie's mother died and Jim asked me to be there for Chrissie, I've truly loved her.

I finally decided that loving the kid had more to do with her than with me. I love her because she's lovable. Okay, Bea, is that so hard to understand?

Thank God for Jeanne. Among Jeanne, Miriam, and me, maybe we could get Chrissie through this. How could that miserable excuse for a judge turn that predator loose? I sat for the few more minutes it took to pull myself together.

I got up, unlocked the padlock, opened the door to the basement, found the light switch and walked down the steps to a large, cluttered room that contained all of the junk that I couldn't possibly leave behind when I gave up my condo and moved in with Alex. On top of my junk, there was Alex's junk, which he had no further use for but couldn't possibly throw out. And on top of that was *our* junk. Maybe we should have a yard sale. Or, more feasibly, call a junk dealer.

Behind me, I heard the door bang shut. Wind? Then I heard the padlock click. Not wind. I walked back up the steps and pushed the door. It remained firmly shut.

I sat down on the steps. This was a fine howdoyoudo, albeit not a serious howdoyoudo. I looked at my watch. Alex should be back in about twenty minutes. I'll start banging on the door in fifteen minutes. When Alex doesn't find me in the house, he'll come out to the patio, hear the noise, and let me out.

But why would someone lock me in the basement? Unless he planned to set the house on fire and fry me. Now that was an uncomfortable thought. But why would someone want to fry me? Maybe I should start banging on the door now.

I ran up the stairs and banged some more. Then I ran back down the stairs and paced. Finally, I sat back down and cautioned myself not to panic. Then I panicked, ran back up the stairs and hollered for help. That was as efficacious as the banging. I sat back down again and put my head in my hands. After about ten minutes, and no flames appeared, I decided to look for the summer shorts.

I had my head in the trunk when I heard the door open. "Hey, Bea, you okay?"

I ran up the stairs to find Johnny Notte. He was standing there with a metal clipper in one hand and the broken padlock in the other.

"I'm fine. Thanks for rescuing me. How'd you know I was in there?"

"I'll tell ya inna minute. Dere's a note onna door."

I looked. The note said, 'Last warning. Back off.'

"Back off what?" I yelped.

Johnny looked disgusted. "Goddam amateur's tryin' a play in a professional league. Don' worry aboud it. I'll take care a it."

Alex came out on the patio and joined us. He was holding a package of cream cheese.

"What's going on?"

Johnny said, "I was lookin' out my back winnow an' I see a guy jumpin' over your back fence. He locked Bea inna basement, stuck a note onna door, an' ran back da way he came.

"So I got da clipper an' came inna same way he did an' let her out. I'da got here sooner but I hadda find the clippers and run aroun' da block ta get ta your yard. Da cedar fence is too high ta jump."

"Geez!" Alex said. "Do you know what this is all about?"

"Yeah. I t'ink so. Don' worry. I'll fix it."

"Did you recognize the guy?" I asked.

Johnny grinned. "Don' worry. I'll fix it."

I said, "Okay. We won't worry. We're about to have breakfast. Do you want to get Marilyn and join us?"

"Naw, t'anks anyway. I gotta make a phone call. Okay if I go t'rough your house?"

Johnny walked through the house whistling 'When a felon's not engaged in his employment...'

Alex and I looked at one another. The Mafia meets Gilbert and Sullivan. Would you believe?

We sat down to our lox and bagels.

Alex asked, "Are you sure you aren't into something that someone wants you out of?"

"I'd be the first to know. The only remotely possible thing would be identifying the guy who stole the reagents and we've already done that."

Alex swallowed a bite of bagel. "You think maybe that nutty Ethel..."

I shook my head. "I can't believe that Ethel the Useless is behind this. The klutz would have broken her neck jumping over the fence and besides, Johnny said it was a guy."

Alex thought about it. "Johnny said something about amateurs in a professional league. Maybe it *is* someone who's trying to make Cody Kletsch's murder look like a mob hit."

"That's the only explanation that comes to mind. And if that's the case, Johnny will certainly take care of it. It's convenient having a friendly, concerned mobster living next door."

While we were cleaning up the breakfast mess, Alex asked if I had found the summer clothes. I confessed that I had not.

Together, we went down to the basement. We found the exercise shorts, among other things, in the trunk. Rummaging farther, Alex pulled out a long, black, hooded garment. It was wrapped around a full face mask. White with red lips and fangs.

"What's this?"

"It's a vampire costume," I said.

Silence. Then, "May I ask what a vampire costume is doing in the trunk?"

"Oh," I said. "The trunk was Harry's and mine."

"And?"

"OK. The jig is up. Harry was an archeologist. He taught a class at UMD and he was taking his students on a nearby teaching dig. They had some of the pits dug before quitting for the weekend. So naturally, Harry and I went to the costume store and bought the vampire clothes."

"Of course, naturally," said Alex, laughing.

"Well, it seemed the natural thing to do at the time," I said.

I went on. "Anyway, we took the costume home, stuffed it to simulate a body inside the clothes, and snuck the assemblage into one of the pits. I don't think Harry's students will ever forget the experience."

"Geez," said Alex. "I wish I'da been there."

We got the summer clothes out of the trunk without further incident.

As we headed out to the car Alex cried, "Whoa! Jim and Jeanne are getting married tomorrow. Don't we need dress-up clothes?"

Whoops. We ran back into the house and looked for appropriate garb. I settled on a calf-length green sheath. This did not require much thought since it was the only appropriate thing in my closet. I'm not much on fashion.

The same can be said of Alex, who owns a grand total of one suit and one dress shirt. The tie caused an agony of indecision. He owns two of those.

Alex revved up the Mustang and we took off. "You up for a limerick?" he asked.

"If you have a limerick" I replied. "hit me with it."

"*A young computernik known as Mad Matt.*"

"Come on, Alex. We're supposed to lay off the math for a while."

"So?" said Alex. "A computernik isn't a mathematician. And besides, one line doesn't make a limerick. If you don't like it, fix it."

"Alright, buster. How's this? *Crying, 'Genetics is where it's all at'*"

"Genetics? You're reaching too far."

I gloated. "What you really mean is you can't think of the next lines. I'll give you a choice. Would you prefer Cajun or

Creole?"

"Don't count your chickens. *Crossed a Ford veep whom he knew, with a small mammal that flew.* Cincinnati or Texas chile, dear heart?"

"This ain't no chicken. *And wound up with an auto.exec.bat.*"

Alex burst out laughing and nearly ran us off the road.

As we turned onto the road to LIT, we saw a man standing in front of the newly painted shed, admiring a sign saying "Buddy's Place."

Could that be *our* Buddy? The guy who ran the grocery store in Alexandria? The man turned around. It not only could be, it was. Buddy was not just the proprietor of the grocery store we frequented, but he was also a friend. On the days when his dad was minding the store, he often had dinner at our house. That's what he was doing the day I got myself mushroom poisoned.[4] Well, I didn't exactly get myself mushroom poisoned. Someone else got me mushroom poisoned. Alex and Buddy took me to the hospital where I spent the night drinking liquid charcoal and cursing my fate.

Buddy is a gangly, tow headed man in his early thirties. About once a month he visits us at the cabin and provides over-the-hill apples for the alpacas.

Alex turned into the parking lot. We got out of the car and ran up to Buddy.

"What are you doing here?" Alex asked.

---

[4]See A Fine Climate for Murder

Buddy laughed. "Well, you know, I'm thinking about getting married..."

I said, "You've been thinking about getting married for over a year. We still haven't met your beloved."

"Yeah. But now I'm *really* thinking about it. And my kid brother, Kevin, is about to finish high school and he wants to help in the store. So we decided to expand our operation. Whenever I came this way, I noticed this location and when that alligator place went out of business, I thought it would be a good place for a grocery store.

"And if I'm going to get married..."

"Are you?" Alex asked. "Or are you still just thinking about it."

"Well," said Buddy, "since Pru said 'yes', I guess I'm getting married."

"When?" Alex and I said.

Buddy grinned. "January. We'll send you an invitation."

"I should hope so," Alex said.

Buddy chortled. "Anyway, here I am. C'mon in and sit down."

We entered the mostly empty shed and sat on some folding chairs.

Buddy explained, "We're going to stock the place with as much local stuff as we can get. I've already talked to some of the farmers. The produce is mostly seasonal but a lot of the farms have honey and jam and preserves and baked goods. Right now, the plan is to stay open year-round, but we may close in the winter. Or we may just close on week-ends in the winter. We're planning to put in a book rack so if we're open and the road isn't safe, people can sit around and read until the plow comes through.

"I made arrangements with some of the county libraries. They all have fifty cent books for sale. You know, the books that have gone a while without being taken out, so the library runs a sale to make room for more books. I can buy some of the books from the sale and sell them here for seventy five cents. Good deal all around.

"Also, there's more land for sale next to my store. We're trying to interest someone into buying it and opening a complementary place."

Alex and I stared at him. "No porn!" we cried.

Buddy looked startled. "Why would I want a porn shop next door? No. I'm talking to someone who might want to open a sandwich shop. He wants to sell wine and beer, too, and I don't want him to."

"Why not?" Alex asked.

"Same reason I'm not selling alcohol here. We're right on the highway and if someone comes in, buys a couple of six packs, starts drinking, and has a serious accident, I'd feel responsible. I don't need that on my conscience."

Alex said, "Good point. But how can you stop someone from selling alcohol?"

Buddy grinned. "Bella Villa County has a regulation that says you can't sell alcohol unless your next door neighbors agree to it. No way am I gonna agree.

"Anyway, Pru and I have been looking for a little house in

Bella Villa."

"And you never told us," I complained.

"Nope," said Buddy, "we wanted to surprise you. Are you surprised?"

"And how!" Alex said.

Just as we got up to continue on our way, the door opened and a diminutive blonde walked in, followed by two guys carrying a couch.

The blonde directed the guys to put the couch about eight feet from the back wall. When it was settled facing the wall, she declared herself satisfied and the two guys left.

Buddy introduced Pru, who explained the placement of the couch. "We're going to put in a gas fireplace and if we put it near the back wall, the gas line from the propane tank won't have to run very far."

She turned to Buddy, got up in her toes, and kissed his chin.

We wished the two of them the best and drove off.

"Did you notice," Alex said, "that the lady is stacked?"

"Thanks for pointing that out."

Eventually, we arrived at LIT, where Alex addressed the expectant multitude.

A young computernik known as Mad Matt,
Crying, Genetics is where it's all at,
Crossed a Ford veep, whom he knew,
With a small mammal that flew,
And wound up with an auto.exec.bat

It goes without saying. Cheers, applause, and general satisfaction.

Don and I went off down the admin corridor. "How goes the remodeling, Don?"

"It doesn't."

Without prodding, Don was clearly not going to say another word.

"Why doesn't it?"

"Because," Don growled, "the effing contractor went bankrupt."

"In the middle of your job? What a mess!."

"That's not the worst."

Well I've pulled the back teeth. Let's start on the incisors. "What is the worst, Don?"

"Connie told me not to hire these guys in the first place."

"Why?"

"She said I'm always hiring cheap-os and then regretting it."

"Is that true?"

"Yeah," said Don and walked on toward his office.

Knowing Don, my guess is that he'll continue to hire cheap-os and that he'll continue to regret it.

Jim and Jeanne were sitting in my office, waiting for me.

"How's Chrissie doing?" I asked.

"Mostly okay," Jeanne answered. "She's pretending that everything's fine, that it could have been worse. We didn't think that coming to work was such a hot idea, but she really wants to pick up the threads of her life. God, I wish I hadn't let her walk back by herself."

"Don't kick yourself around, Jeanne. The scumbag was obviously stalking her. If you had been with her he would just have waited for another time. And it would probably have been a time when Sam and Joe weren't there to break it up."

I wondered if they knew that Jimboy the Lesser had walked. Should I tell them? No. At least not yet. They have enough on their plate.

Jim said, "She also insisted that we keep our wedding date on Saturday. Says she wants everything to be as normal as possible."

Jeanne added, "Says she'll be darned if she'll let her 'stupid trauma' interfere with her life."

I laughed. "That's my Chrissie."

Jim said, "We're lucky we didn't plan a big wedding. Just you two. We did adjust the arrangements a little. `Still scheduled for 10:30, but we asked Father Haydn if we could move the ceremony to his office. Explained about Chrissie and that we were concerned that someone might come into the church and maybe upset her. He understood right away. He agreed that there was no telling how she'd react to a stranger walking in on the ceremony. Or how she'd react to the ceremony even if no one walked in. Best to move to the office.

"We talked to Ralph and Miriam. She thinks that the wedding will be pretty emotional for Chrissie, so they'll wait for us after the ceremony and Chrissie will go home with them. They didn't want to join us in the office. Miriam thought more people might make it harder on Chrissie.

"We wanted to cancel, but Chrissie insisted that Jeanne and I take our scheduled three-day honeymoon. So she'll stay with the Manleys through Monday night and then on Tuesday she'll either go to LIT with Ralph or stay home with Miriam, depending on how well she's doing."

"After that, " Jeanne added, "we wanted to ask you if you'd keep an eye on Chrissie for a while. She's had a flashback and we're afraid there may be more. She refuses to talk to a counselor – doesn't want to 'share her problems with a stranger'. And we're afraid that if we hover too closely, she'll resent us."

I said, "Of course I'll keep an eye on her. But I wouldn't worry about her resenting you. Rape or no rape, she's a sensible kid. My guess is she'll be as worried about you as you are about her."

Jim and Jeanne departed.

There was a note on my desk telling me to call Ted Papageorge at the Department. He was a stupidly officious jerk who usually meant trouble. I called.

"Come my office tomorrow morning," he said. "I've got problems with your budget submission."

I closed my eyes. "Give me a hint, Ted, so I'm sure to bring the right material."

"You've got too much money allocated for supplies. We can cut your budget there."

"This is a Lab, Ted. We aren't talking about pencils and

paper. We're talking about lab equipment and experimental technology."

"Save the argument for tomorrow. I'll expect you at nine."

I hung up the phone, gently. Ted reported to the Assistant Secretary for Administration, Catherine Waite. Cate Waite lived on my block in Alexandria. I looked up her number in the Federal Directory.

"Assistant Secretary Waite's office."

"Good morning. This is Dr. Beatrice Goode. Would Ms. Waite be available to talk with me?"

"Please hold."

The next voice I heard was Cate's. "Hey, Bea. What's going on?"

"Ted Papageorge."

"Oh, God. What's that fool done now?"

"He thinks we're spending too much money on lab equipment. He wants me in his office tomorrow morning."

"The ass is going to get us cross-wise with Dr. Lee, isn't he?"

"Yep."

"Which will get me cross-wise with the Secretary, won't it?"

"Yep."

"I don't know what I'm going to do with that imbecile."

"How did you get him in the first place?"

"I inherited him. It's too much trouble to fire anyone so people kept promoting him to get him out of their hair. Now he's up as far as he can go and I'm stuck with him."

"So what do you want me to do?" I asked.

"Nothing. Don't keep the appointment. I'll take care of it."

I hung up and laughed. Johnny Notte ain't the only guy who can take care of things.

I walked to my morning meeting with Pie and Don, leaving the rest of my inbox until later.

The first part of the meeting was devoted to the impending session with OMB. The first part of that segment was divided in two subsections. First, what should Pie's role be? The BioCenter's presenters, Adrienne Hodler – if not off producing a baby – and Molly Cameron were more than capable of wowing the inquisitors. But the eminent microbiologist, Dr. P.I. Lee, would be expected to weigh in. Decision was to pass the buck. Pie would huddle with Adrienne and Molly.

Then came the discussion of what should be done if Adrienne were to be the primary presenter and went into labor in the middle of it all. The three of us agreed that it would certainly make for an interesting presentation. 'Shall we adjourn for a water break?' We also agreed that I should be the one to transport her to the hospital. If the occasion arises, Don will call Sam and arrange an escort.

Those weighty matters decided, we moved on to my morning's adventures.

The narration left Pie incredulous and Don mightily amused.

"Let me see if I understand this," Pie said. "Some *shtunk* locked you into a well lighted, well ventilated place where you wanted to be anyway, shortly before you expected your husband to come looking for you. But even before Alex could get home with the combination to the padlock, a *mentsch* of a mafioso cut the padlock and let you out, also pointing to a note telling you to stop doing something that you didn't know you were doing. Is that correct?"

"Yes. That's a fair statement."

"D'ya think," said Don, "that this could be Molly getting even with you?"

Pie and I both exploded with laughter. When I stopped laughing, I said "I don't think so, Don. First of all, dead rats are hardly Molly's style. Second, I don't see Molly scaling the back fence. And more to the point, I think Johnny recognized the culprit."

"What was it you quoted?" Don asked. 'Once you have eliminated the impossible, whatever remains, however improbable, must be true.' Well, I agree that it's improbable that Molly might clamber over your back fence..."

At which picture all three of us broke up.

We went on to clear up some of the trivia that the Department had visited upon us, and then repaired to the lunch room. We were just finishing our cobblers when we spotted Ralph Manley and Chrissie heading toward us with full trays. We moved over to make room for them. Pie said, "Hello, Ralph. Hello, Chrissie. I'm glad to see you back at LIT. How are you doing?"

"I think I'll survive. I wasn't so sure yesterday. But everyone's been great. The Center has been like family.

"Doctor Goode, could I come and talk to you for a few minutes after lunch?"

"Sure. I just finished dessert so I'll get back to my office, deal with the last of the trivia, and wait for you."

Pie, Don and I left.

Within half an hour, Chrissie appeared. "Dr. Goode, do you know Blake Halonen?"

"Not well, but I know who he is."

"He told me he loved me. And I thought about what Mrs. Manley said and that you heard her say it. Did you put Blake up to it?"

"I wouldn't say that I put him up to it. But he told me he was in love with you and I suggested that he tell you. Was that the wrong thing to do?" So alright, I left a few things out.

"No!" Chrissie said quickly. "He's a very nice guy." And she broke into tears. After a while she said, "I've been crying a lot lately. I don't like it."

I gave her a hug. "You can come in here and cry any time you feel a sob-session coming on."

She hugged me back and went off to her lab.

A few minutes later, Ben walked in. "Did you see Maureen Bunyan's noon broadcast?"

"No. What was on it?"

Ben said, "The *putz* who raped Chrissie was found beaten half to death on the judge's doorstep."

"Good grief! Did they catch who did it?"

"No, thank God. I hope they never do."

"Any other details?

"Just that both kneecaps were smashed, his, uh, genitals had been interfered with, and a great many bones have been broken."

"Nothing about the trial?"

"Oh yes," Ben said. "Bunyan went on about that at length. How the slime bag of a judge just let him go. And that the poor scuzzbucket said he felt just terrible that he wasn't able to protect Chrissie.

"Well," Ben continued, "now he's *really* broken up about it." Ben left.

I had just finished dealing with my inbox when a tap came on my half-open door. I looked up and discovered Bessie. "What a nice surprise! Is this a way stop on your travels to Pie's office?"

"No. I'm here to see you." Bessie closed the door behind her. "Are you okay, Bea?"

We both sat down. There was no sense pretending that I didn't know what she meant. She knows me too well.

"I could use a hug."

Bessie got up and obliged. She and Pie were old friends of my former husband's parents, neither of whom were still alive when I met and married Harry. Pie and Bessie would have been godparents to Harry's and my kids. Then, as Harry and I drove home from the movies one evening, we got creamed by a drunk driver. Harry was killed. I had a miscarriage. I can't have children.

Bessie and Pie have always been there for me. When Alex

was shot and almost died, it was Bessie who got me through it. She has a pretty good idea of how much Chrissie means to me. She and Pie are childless by choice. But by choice or not, I think most women, at least some of the time, want to mother a kid. And there's something to be said for mothering a mature kid. None of the inconvenience of smelly diapers and unspeakable adolescence. At any rate, Bessie has had me to mother, and ever since Chrissie's mother died and Jim asked me to help Chrissie cope, I've had Chrissie.

I looked down at my hands. "I'd like to take Chrissie under my wing and mother her. But it's important that she rely on Jeanne. Who, by the way, also loves her."

Bessie thought a bit. "Do you think Jeanne might resent your closeness to Chrissie?"

"No. Jeanne is one of the most level-headed, equable people I've ever met. She understands perfectly well that because someone –in this case, Chrissie – loves someone it doesn't diminish the love felt for someone else."

Bessie smiled. "And you aren't jealous of her?"

"Jealous of Jeanne? No. I don't think so." I thought. "No. I know so."

I went on, "I think, to be jealous of someone you sort of have to put yourself in that person's shoes so that you know what you're jealous of. Does that make sense?"

"Not much," Bessie said, "but continue anyway."

"Well, I'm very fond of Jim, but I couldn't possibly be jealous of someone who would marry him. If for no other reason than that he'd probably show up for the wedding in his Einstein mask."

Bessie and I looked at one another. She said, "You don't think...."

I said, "The priest would probably excommunicate him."

We both burst out laughing.

In the middle of the hilarity, Pie knocked and entered. "Hey, Bessie. Lenore said you were here. What's so funny?

Bessie and I got ourselves under control.

Bessie said, "It's a girl thing, Pie. You wouldn't understand."

I thought about going to the Forensic Lab but decided to settle for a phone call. Paul took the call right away. There was no need for me to come in; I could learn all there was to know over the phone. Jazz had looked at everything she knew to be Cody's work. Nothing jumped out, except that Elliott Giles' Black ancestry was confirmed. It also appeared that Cody had looked at Jazz's material. Nothing out of the ordinary in it, but Jazz told Paul that it would be okay if someone else also looked at it. In fact, she would welcome it.

"Who do you think killed Cody, Bea?"

"I haven't a clue. Each of the team members has a motive, but they've had the motive for quite some time. Unless Cody recently upped Giles' blackmail payments – which is a definite possibility – there's no apparent reason to kill Cody now."

Paul sighed. "I certainly hope none of them did it. I may be able to save the Lab if it's an outside perpetrator. I don't think I can pull it off if one of us did it."

He rang off at the same time that Don walked in. Lenore had told him and Pie about Maureen Bunyan's noon broadcast and had provided some details that Ben left out.

Jimboy the First was both inconsolable and vowing vengeance. He seemed particularly upset about the damage to Jimboy the Lesser's genitals. He might never be able to rape again. The judge had barricaded himself in his house, terrified that he might be the next target. And in a later bulletin: calls were pouring in to the station -- all but one of them applauding the vigilante action as well as demanding the judge's immediate removal from the bench. The single dissenter thought that prosecution for rape was a prime example of government interference in private matters.

Jimboy the Lesser had moments of clarity, but not many. He didn't know who did it. He had parked his car in the judge's driveway and was on his way to the judge's house to thank him for his consideration. A sack had been dropped over his head. He didn't see his assailants. He said that he thought there were three of them. Then he thought there were four. Then he thought there was only one. And that was all he remembered.

I asked, "Who do you think did it, Don?"

"Dunno. No lack of candidates. Do you think it might have been Joe?"

"Could be. He was angry enough," I answered. "If it was, I doubt if he'll be caught. Sam will be in charge of the investigation. I'd be amazed if he failed to protect Joe."

Don nodded. "And more power to him! But what about the trio?"

"Definite possibility. But still no way that Sam would collar them. And besides, they'll get alibied by every music lover in Shaw. 'Why officer, those nice boys were playing for us all night'. And good on them!

"Just as likely is that Johnny Notte's telephone call resulted in immediate action."

Don looked skeptical. "You saying that the mob might have made the hit on the scuzzbucket but you believe the mob *didn't* hit that guy from the Forensic Lab?"

I nodded. "That's exactly what I'm saying. In any case, I doubt if we'll ever know."

"Unless," Don said, "the scuzzbucket remembers how many of the attackers were involved. You know, one if by Joe, two if by Notte...."

I shook my head. "That confusion is a result of trauma. You get the same thing with traumatized war vets. Different, conflicting images present themselves to their brains. And then look at Chrissie. She's confused about who raped her – despite the fact that she must have seen the scuzzbucket in The Rabbit Hole.

"That's why juries fail to convict so many rapists. The victim gets on the stand and produces inconsistent testimony. The jury notices that the narrative doesn't add up and concludes that the woman is lying."

"Bea," said Don, "are you trying to tell me that every rape acquittal is wrong?"

"Not at all. I'm sure some acquittals are entirely justified. What I am telling you is that a woman's inconsistent testimony shouldn't be the sole basis for acquittal. Prosecutors too often fail to bring up the effects of trauma on the victim's memory."

Don thought about it. "I didn't know about that. I'm glad Chrissie didn't have to testify."

I nodded. "If the slimebag hadn't waived the jury trial, the cross examination would have been devastating for Chrissie. Even if the jury convicted."

Alex and I were motoring up the driveway when we noted both the junior Cokers' truck and Sam's squad car in front of the Coker's house. Claudia was in the road, flagging us down.

"Come on in," she said. "We're having an impromptu dinner party. Sam was telling us about what happened to that horrible rapist."

Never ones to turn down a dinner at the Cokers, we abandoned the Mustang and joined them.

Alex asked, "Did you catch the guys who beat up the scumbag?"

"Naw," said Sam. "Not likely to." He offered a sly smile. "Victim's testimony was so inconsistent, if it weren't for the injuries we'd have thought he made it up."

Alex and I both laughed. "Not Joe, huh?" I inquired.

"No, no, no," Sam answered. "He was on patrol with Walt and me all night. Couldn't have done it."

"How about the trio?"

"Gracious no," Sam said. "They were nowhere near Maryland. Playing at a private party in the District."

"Well, then," Alex said, "it must have been the Mafia."

"Not necessarily." Sam was at his most judicious. "The scumbag may have had enemies we know nothing about. Given that he's a scumbag, that's quite likely. Unless something turns up, we'll just have to admit it's insoluble.

"The guy's daddy has been vowing to launch his own Congressional investigation and get me impeached, or whatever they do to naughty sheriffs, but I don't think that'll happen."

"What makes you think that?" Big Daryl asked.

Young Daryl responded, "Can you see a Congressional Committee getting put in the position of defending a rapist? Aside from the fact that a Congressional Committee can't impeach a county official, Bella Villa County would just vote Sam back into office. It won't happen."

Sandy piped up. "I really don't think vigilante justice is a good way to go, but when you've got a crooked judge, that's the only justice you're going to get."

"Amen to that," I said.

"Enough of this," Claudia pronounced. "Let's eat. We've got steaks on the grill."

As we sat around the dinner table, I gave them as much of the Forensic Lab's tribulations as they needed to know in order to answer the burning question.

"Sandy, the murdered man owned a silver Labrador retriever. He's still a puppy – about a year old. Would you and Junior consider adopting him?"

"What's a silver Lab?" Sandy asked.

Sam actually knew the answer. "A friend of mine has one. The color has something to do with the variation in their genes. The American Kennel Club recognizes that they're real Labs, but classifies them as chocolate Labs. My friend's dog has yellow eyes. He is one good looking dog."

The young Cokers thought about it. "We've got enough space for him to run," Junior said. "Can we meet him?"

"I'm sure that can be arranged. But in case you don't already know it, Labrador retrievers are usually terrible puppies before they become great dogs. The pups jump on everyone. They chew up everything. They laser in on any food left uncovered. You just have to wait out the puppyhood."

"That's not a problem," Sandy said. "We really do have enough space for the dog to burn off the excess energy."

Sam piped up. "Even if it doesn't work out with Sandy and Junior, one of my deputies might take him."

That settled, Alex and I finished dinner, thanked the Cokers for a wonderful meal, and departed for the cabin.

Chrissie's Taurus was in front of the cabin, pulled up on the grass in order to leave room for the Mustang. Chrissie, herself, was seated on the front step. She stood up as we got out of the car. Alex greeted her. "Come on in, Chris."

She followed us in. We all sat down; Chrissie and I on the couch, Alex in the easy chair.

I asked, "How come your car is here? Didn't you drive to

LIT with Jim and Jeanne?"

"No," she answered. "I wasn't sure I could make it through the day and I didn't want to make Daddy and Jeanne leave early. So I came in my car."

She waited a few beats, took a big breath, and said. "I'd like to ask you a big favor."

Alex said, "Sure."

I said, "Of course."

Chrissie said. "Could I come here tomorrow morning, get dressed, and go with you to the ceremony?"

Alex said, "That's a big favor? Sure you can come."

I said, "That doesn't even rank as a little favor. We'd be happy to take you."

Chrissie said, "The thing is, I don't know from one minute to the next what I'm going to do. It's like I'm sitting somewhere above me and watching the other me behaving like an idiot. So I say to me, 'Don't behave like an idiot' and then I go right on behaving like an idiot.

"I'm pretty sure that I can hold myself together during the ceremony but I don't know what I'll do earlier, in the morning. And I don't want to ruin the day for Daddy and Jeanne."

Alex said, "Would you be upset if I came over there and gave you a hug?"

Chrissie laughed. "I don't know, try it."

Alex tried it. Chrissie wasn't upset.

Alex came back to the couch and gave *me* a hug for good measure. He's good at that.

"One of the big problems," Chrissie went on, "is that I'm terrified that he'll get out of jail and come after me again."

Alex and I looked at one another.

"What is it?" Chrissie asked. "Is he out?"

"Only in a manner of speaking," Alex said.

I wasn't sure how much to tell Chrissie, but I finally opted for full disclosure.

Chrissie stared at me. "Oh my God. Oh my God."

Then she burst into tears. Then she laughed.

"You mean my avenger is either a cop, or some boys from the 'hood, or a gangster?"

She started laughing again. "Wait'll I tell Blake!"

And having dropped that bombshell, she left.

CHAPTER 9
May 29 - 30, 1993

We peered out the door to encounter another perfect day and a basket of tomatoes on our doorstep. Bless the Cokers and their over-abundant garden.

"Alex, is there any more of that sharp cheddar in the fridge?"

"I think so. Lemme look."

As I was turning to go back inside, I heard Chrissie's Taurus pull up.

Alex wandered back. "Lots of cheddar and enough bread for hot ones."

I glanced out the window as Chrissie was opening the trunk and extracting a dress bag and a pair of stylish shoes. She was dressed in jeans, a tee, and a backpack.

I opened the door and ushered her in.

"Good morning, Dr. Goode. Hi, Dr. Carfil."

Alex smiled at her. "Have you had breakfast?"

"Just coffee."

"In that case," I said, "sit down with us. We were about to make hot ones."

"Okay. Whatever a hot one is. I trust you." She dropped her burdens.

I explained. "A hot one is an open-faced sandwich loaded

with sharp cheddar cheese, a slice of tomato, a sprinkling of oregano from the herb garden, salt, and pepper. You shove the sandwich under the broiler until the cheese starts to melt."

Alex relieved Chrissie of her burdens while I started the hot ones.

Alex put on the coffee, Chrissie set the table, and we began the meal. After the first bite, Chrissie said, "See, I knew I could trust you."

"How are you doing?" Alex asked.

Chrissie swallowed. "Not too bad. The nights are horrible, though. I keep waking up in a cold sweat. Mrs. Manley said that will pass so I can put up with it. I don't think I could if I thought it would go on forever. I can get through the day okay. I had a flashback and that was awful. And I keep crying. I understand that this is normal, but I *hate* being a stereotype. At least I'm not having problems with eating."

She swallowed the last of her hot one and went to get another.

Alex and I couldn't help it. We laughed. Chrissie withdrew her head from the oven. She was laughing, too.

Chrissie and I went into the bedroom to change. Alex went into the bathroom to do the same. Except for the tie. He'd need help with the tie.

Chrissie said, "I wonder why men have trouble with ties. Daddy does too. I mean, men get lots of practice but they never get it right. Women don't wear ties, but they always know how to tie them straight. Strange."

She divested herself of jeans, tee, socks, and sneakers. Took pantyhose from the backpack and a scoop-neck, soft, rose, calf-length, dress from the dress bag and assembled them on herself. I followed a similar procedure with the green sheath.

I inspected Chrissie. "You, my dear, are gorgeous. The dress is perfect."

Chrissie gave me the once over. "You're not so bad yourself, Dr. Goode."

We hugged. There came a knocking on the door. "Bea? Can you help me with the tie?"

Chrissie opened the door. Alex took one look at her and said, "Wow!"

Chrissie grinned. "Wait'll you see me with my make-up in place." She grabbed the backpack and made for the bathroom.

Alex looked like a kid about to go on his first date. The suit was impeccable. The shirt was white and crisp. His dress-up shoes were shined to perfection. But then there was the tie. It looked like it had been knotted by a cock-eyed kangaroo.

I re-tied Alex's tie. I didn't get it right either.

Chrissie returned, took one look at Alex, and said, "Oh, for pity's sake." She grabbed him by the tie and proceeded to re-do it. Humbled, I went to apply my own make-up.

Father Haydn's living quarters and office were located next to the church. His housekeeper answered the door and ushered us into the office. Jim and Jeanne were not there yet. The office was a large room, comfortably furnished with a rather ornate desk, a couch and a number of stuffed chairs. A fireplace, sandwiched between two low bookshelves, was on one wall. Above them a crucifix and several prints of the Madonna and child, including a superb thirteenth century work by Duccio di Buoninsegna.

A taller set of book shelves covered another wall. I inspected the contents. A mixture of religious tomes, weighty analyses of current events, and a goodly bunch of thrillers. I looked up. An amused Father Haydn was inspecting my inspection.

He was a pleasant looking man in his late sixties or early seventies. Sweet smile.

He beckoned us to be seated and asked if we would like coffee. No thank you. We were seated on the couch, Chrissie between Alex and me. Where were Jim and Jeanne?

We entered into awkward conversation: covered the weather pretty thoroughly; wondered if Washington would ever get a baseball team; discussed the merits of Perez-Reverte's just published suspense novel, *The Club Dumas.*

Jim and Jeanne rushed in. They had forgotten the marriage license and had to go back to get it. Without it, the ceremony could not proceed. Father Haydn laughed. Chrissie rolled her eyes.

Jim and Jeanne stood before the priest. Father Haydn began the ceremony by saying, "You both realize that we almost never do a wedding outside the church such as here in my office. But you are a special couple." He smiled at them.

"Jeanne and James, have you come here freely..."

As he began, Chrissie grabbed my hand. I glanced at her. Her lips were pressed together. Hang on, Chrissie. Hang on. I squeezed her hand.

"*...join your right hands, and declare your consent...*"

Chrissie moved closer to me.

"*What God has joined, men must not divide.*"

Chrissie locked her fingers in mine.

"*May these rings be a symbol...*"

Jim produced the ring and united it with Jeanne's finger. Jeanne reciprocated.

"*Almighty and Wonderful Father, look with love on Jeanne, your daughter. She asks your blessing...*"

As he finished Jim turned to Jeanne and kissed her. Chrissie took a deep breath, got up and kissed them both.

Alex and I escorted her out to where Ralph and Miriam awaited. By the time we got Chrissie into the back seat, she was shaking. Miriam put her arms around her. They drove off.

We got into the Mustang. Alex loosened the tie, and we headed for the cabin. Alex said, "This has to be hard on Miriam. I know it's been a long time since she was violated, but ...."

I gazed at my husband. Then I thought of Harry, my first love and first husband, now dead. How did I ever get so lucky? The two kindest, most sensitive guys in the world and I had married both of them. I leaned over and gave Alex a smooch on the ear.

He grinned. "By the way, you look smashing in that dress. Well, you look smashing all the time, but you look particularly smashing in that dress..."

"Thank you."

"...and I can hardly wait to take it off of you."

"Then shut up and drive."

After our shower, we reverted to normal clothing. Alex in chinos and a polo shirt; me in jeans and a tee. I wondered what became of Alex's tie. Would he have flushed it down the toilet? Nah.

"You wanna get lunch at The Rabbit Hole?" Alex asked.

"Sounds good. I'd like to go to Bella Villa in any case. I think the trio is there practicing for Memorial Day. Maybe Chuck will let us sneak a peek at the Stump Chuck winner."

The Stump Chuck contest is what birthed the Chuck Hadaman Museum. Chuck is something of a genius with metal work. An example of this is the huge metal llama that stands outside the museum. Kids climb the steps on one side and go down the slide on the other. Other towns have war heroes on horses as monuments. Bella Villa has kids on a llama.

One year, Chuck fabricated something for a homecoming float. That first fabrication showed cheerleaders jumping up and down waving pom poms. That, of course, caused the town to demand a fabrication every year. Not only that, but they started a Stump Chuck contest with football-related entries attempting to describe something that was difficult but not impossible to fabricate. Barely possible was okay. One of the later winning entries, for instance, was a football player, arms pumping, chasing a squealing pig. As it happens, Chuck is no slouch as an electrician.

After a few years, the realizations of the winning entries began to pile up in Mayor Petrofsky's basement and the town decided to create a Chuck Hadaman Museum to display them. Now, a decade from the start, Chuck's museum is a Bella Villa landmark.

Alex and I hopped in the Mustang and headed toward the town, which was in a state of busy excitement. Citizens and their spawn were gathering to construct floats; the high school band was making more-or-less musical noises; and the voice of little kids shrieking was heard in the land. We parked and scooted into The Rabbit Hole. A large metal rabbit served as greeter. Whenever the door opened, the rabbit bowed. Chuck's handiwork. I think Duane paid him in Welsh rabbits.

Chuck was seated at a table for four.

Duane, the restaurant's maitre d', waiter, and proprietor noticed our entrance and dragged another table over to elongate the one where Chuck sat. Chuck got two more chairs.

"The three musicians are w-w-washing up. They'll be here in a minute."

"What's going on?" Alex asked.

"They were helping to put up the new sign. The town re-named the m-m-museum."

"What's the new name?" I asked.

Willis joined us. "It's now the Hadaman Museum of Homecoming Art."

Arthur and Lomas arrived. All sat down and Duane brought the Welsh rabbits and a pitcher of beer. The Rabbit Hole does have a menu with a number of items on it, but I've never heard of anyone ordering anything except a Welsh rabbit. If someone should do so, I have the feeling that Duane would claim the restaurant was out of it.

Whatever it was.

Alex asked Chuck, "Can we get an advance peek at the Stump Chuck winner?"

Chuck shook his head. "You know the r-r-rules."

"What are the rules?" Willis asked.

I answered, "The museum is closed for a week before Memorial Day while Chuck does the fabrication. No one is allowed to enter. Then Sunday night the fabrication is snuck onto a float, which joins the Memorial Day Parade. After the parade, it gets put on its cube in the museum and visitors are admitted. People get a glance while it's on the float, but no one gets a really good look until it's installed in the museum. Right, Chuck?"

"Right."

"But," said Arthur, "we been practicing in the museum and Chuck's not making anything there."

"No," Chuck said. "I'm w-w-working in my garage. But the wiring is getting set up in the museum."

"Okay," Alex said, "now that we know the rules, are you going to let us take a peek?"

Chuck considered. "Did I hear you say you'd m-m-make a donation to the trio's Foundation for instruments for the ghetto kids?"

"That's extortion!" I protested.

Willis smiled. "We never said we were law-abiding citizens."

So we finished our Welsh rabbits and trekked over to Chuck's garage.

Chuck has a little shotgun house, one of several similar houses in Bella Villa. A shotgun house, by the way, has one room following the other in a row, with no impediments that might prevent a bullet from traveling from the entrance to the house to the exit. They are usually associated with Black homes in New Orleans, but a few made their way north and Chuck acquired one of them. Chuck's garage dwarfs his house. Aside from the normal carpentry tools, the space also contains the tools he needs for mold casting, die casting, extrusion, stamping, and Lord only knows what else. But there's a lot of it. A corner of the garage contained this year's winner of the Stump Chuck contest.

The cubes in the museum all measure 4x4x4. The current fabrication measures 3x3x3. It was not going to be easy getting the current work centered on the cube.

"This was a b-b-bugger!" Part of the football field and populated stands were shown. The field and teams were near the bottom of the cube. The stands and scoreboard stretched skyward. Several football players were running in various directions attempting to catch a dog that had run onto the field. After less than a minute, a fan jumped out of the stands and tackled the dog.

Alex watched with his mouth ajar. "Chuck, did you program this?"

Chuck nodded.

"Holy cow! It's awesome."

Alex got the checkbook out of his back pocket, wrote a check for $300, and gave it to Lomas.

We began our stroll to the museum to admire the new sign

and inspect the bandstand. I put my hand on Lomas's arm and motioned him to stop.

"Lomas," I said, "if Flo is bankrolling your Foundation, why are you scrounging for donations?"

Lomas laughed. "You found out who Flo is, huh?'

"Chrissie recognized her suit and Flo confessed."

"It's like this," Lomas said. "We only go to Flo for the big stuff. Give you an example. We got a pianist at Ellington now who's got the potential to be one of the greats. His parents couldn't care less, either about him or his potential. Father's a pusher. Mother's a part time prostitute and a full time junkie. Flo's supporting them to the extent that they stay off the kid's case – they don't know where the kid's living and they don't give a damn. Flo bought a big apartment on Connecticut Avenue and a concert grand to go in it. We moved the kid in there with a nice couple who make sure he eats, sleeps, plays, and practices the way he should. Flo arranged for a top flight teacher to push the kid to reach his potential. That's what Flo does. We scrounge the small stuff. You dig?"

"I dig. Does Flo really have that much money?"

Lomas nodded. "Don't know how much, but I read somewhere that Ralph Lauren's worth about six billion, and Flo's in that league."

Great Scott! That took a minute to digest.

Then I said, "How's the kid with all this? Getting plucked out of his natural habitat and into another world."

"He loves it. We were worried about it at first, but he really loves it. He's still got his friends from Ellington. They sleep over a lot on week-ends. The couple we got gives them lots of space as long as they don't interfere with practice time. It's worked out well."

We caught up with the group and continued on to the museum.

The sign, which sat atop the museum's roof, proclaimed in six-foot high letters that this was the place to see the Hadaman Museum of Homecoming Art.

The front of the museum faced the back of the little bandstand which sat a few yards in front of the building. A standard split curtain covered the front of the bandstand. On each side of the bandstand, an arrangement of curtains was anchored to the building on one end and the bandstand on the other, thus concealing the entrance to the museum door. Three temporary steps would allow the trio to emerge unseen from the museum and reach the bandstand's stage. While everyone was watching the parade, the trio would sneak their instruments onto the stage.

As soon as Chuck's float reached the finish line, he would liberate the fabrication, load it onto a large hand truck, and take it to the back door of the museum, where he and the trio would install it on its cube. The trio would then mount the steps to the stage, warm up, wait for the audience to arrive, and at last would perform the Memorial Day concert. When the concert was complete, the side curtains would open and the throng would be invited into the museum. It was an efficient arrangement.

Alex and I drove back to the cabin and went off to consort

with the alpacas. Greetings were exchanged and apple slices dispensed. The llamas wandered over to partake of the goodies.

"Why do farmers raise sheep when they could raise alpacas?" Alex mused. "Alpaca wool is a good cash crop. It's a lot warmer than sheep wool. And they're cuter, smarter, neater, and cuddlier than sheep." He gave one of the alpacas a cuddle to prove his point.

"Because," I said, "the alpaca farmers don't raise their animals to be eaten. They don't sell the meat, just the wool. Selling the lamb meat is more profitable."

Alex said, "Point taken. I think alpaca meat is eaten in South America."

I nodded. "I hope it never comes to that here, though. The thought of Gertie on a grill is horrifying!"

We gave the animals a parting smooch and wandered over to the little bog that occupies a corner of the property. It was dry as a bone.

"If it doesn't rain soon," Alex said, "the farmers are going to be in trouble. The reservoir can't keep irrigating the farms forever."

"Let's hope that the rain holds off until after the Memorial Day parade and then drenches the area."

We walked back toward the cabin and noticed that the barn door was open. We went in to find Daryl and Claudia doing their barnly chores.

Claudia said, "We're scheduled to shear next weekend. A tad late this year. Are you game to help?"

"Absolutely!" Alex said.

"Is alpaca meat eaten anywhere except South America, do

you know?" I asked.

"Yep," Daryl said. "In Australia. Alpacas are mostly bred for the wool, like here, but some alpacas are being used for meat. A few restaurants offer it."

Claudia added, "The meat is called Viande."

I shuddered.

Sunday dawned sunny and clear. Alex and I went out to tend our little herb garden and just as we were thinking of going back inside for a therapeutic snooze, Sam drove up. He said, "My informers have reported that Chuck gave you a look at the Stump Chuck winner. Would you care to share the knowledge?"

"It'll cost you three hundred bucks," Alex said. "They extorted payment to the trio's Foundation."

Sam considered. "I can wait until tomorrow."

He joined us for coffee and cookies in the cabin.

If you've ever seen, or watched a re-run of the Andy Griffith Show, in which Griffith plays the Sheriff of Mayberry, North Carolina, then you know what Sam looks like. He's a dead ringer for Griffith. I've often wondered if that was why Sam decided to run for sheriff in the first place.

Alex brought out the coffee pot and we sat down to drink and munch.

Sam pulled what looked like a telephone out of his pocket. "Looky what I got," he said. "It's a portable phone."

"Do all the deputies have them?" Alex asked.

Sam shook his head. "Wish they did, but they cost nearly

nine hundred bucks. We've got three of them. I carry this one and any deputy who expects to be out of our jurisdiction can pick up one of the others. Problem is that each jurisdiction has its own frequency and we can't radio-talk to each other. But we can communicate using the portable phones."

Alex, who had been fiddling with the gadget, surrendered it. "The price'll come down sooner or later," he said.

Sam returned the phone to his pocket where it made a considerable bulge. "We'll tell the bad guys to stay in radio range until then."

Speaking around a mouthful of almond meringue, I asked if there was any progress in apprehending Jimboy the Lesser's attackers. I knew full well what the answer would be.

"No. It's destined to be a cold case. The scuzzbag is still in intensive care in the hospital. He's not expected to die, but they don't know yet what the permanent damage will be."

Sam swallowed some coffee and asked, "Do you know if any progress has been made on finding that forensic guy's killer?"

I shook my head. "He was killed near his house in Alexandria. He had a couple of acres at the edge of the city, not too far from the county line, so the Alexandria police are handling it.

"It's an odd coincidence that Alexandria has three households connected to this case. Alex and I live in Old Town. Cody lived near the county border. And Adam Brattice had a sort-of estate in the city. He paid over two million for a lovely 1870 house and restored it beautifully. He didn't go in for ostentation. I've seen a picture of the house. He left the original clean lines – didn't add any ain't-I-great frills. His wife and son are living in it now, along with his brother Howard who is probably the kid's biological poppa."

A light bulb went on over my head. "That's what changed!" I exclaimed.

"Would you care to explain?" Sam asked.

"The question was why Cody would be killed now. So far as we know, all the people who have motives have had the motives for years. Something must have changed. I just realized that what changed was that Adam's remains were found."

"But why kill the forensic guy?" Sam asked reasonably.

The same light bulb illuminated Alex. He answered, "If Adam wasn't the kid's biological father, then the kid wouldn't inherit the Brattice fortune and his mother wouldn't be his guardian. The billions would probably go to Adam's sister. It's odds on that the 'forensic guy' was bribed to destroy the evidence and declare Adam to be the father."

I stuck my two cents in. "Cody was into the Mafia for much money in gambling debt. He was desperate for money. As Counselor to the mob, Howard would have known that and therefore known that Cody was bribable. It was probably Howard and the cheating wife who bribed him to declare that Adam was the father."

Sam added, "And then killed him to make sure his mouth stayed shut."

"A stupid move," I said. "It led to Jazz reviewing Cody's work and uncovering the fraud."

"Brilliant deductions," Sam said. "God only knows how to

prove it."

Alex got up to get more coffee. A shout of "Oh, crap!" came from the kitchen and Alex entered the living room, *sans* coffee. "I just realized that I forgot to bring the disks I was working on. I need them for work on Tuesday. I'm going to have to go and get them."

"Not to worry. It's a beautiful day for a top-down drive. I'll go with you." I turned to Sam. "If you're not on duty, would you like to join us? We can have lunch at *Le Gaulois*."

Sam said. "I just came off duty. Sure, I'll join you."

We dumped the dishes in the sink, got in the Mustang, and took off.

We got out of the car and Alex ran up the steps. Sam and I stretched our legs and waited on the sidewalk for him. Johnny came out and joined us. I introduced him to Sam, who was still in uniform. The two men eyed each other uncomfortably.

Johnny said, "I jus' wanned a tell you that two a my, uh, associates paid a visit to da Congressman. You know, to offer sympathies for what happen' a his son. He's very upset as you can well imagine. Said he was gonna resign from Congress to go back home an' help his wife take care a da kid."

"Is that so?" said Sam.

"Yeah. I know he was sayin' dat he was gonna get even. But dat was jus' talk. No one has to worry about dat no more. It was a pleasure meetin' you, sir."

Johnny turned and ran back up to his front door.

Alex came out, carrying a box of disks. He looked

quizzically at the departing Johnny.

Sam said, straight-faced, "He seems a pleasant enough fellow."

We finished up lunch at *Le Gaulois* and were entering the Mustang when Sam asked, "Is Brattice's house nearby?"

"Not too far," I answered. "It's a little north of here, up Apostolic Road. Would you guys like to drive past it?"

Receiving two affirmatives, I turned the car in that direction. As we approached the Brattice house, Sam remarked that there seemed to be quite a bit of money living on the street.

"No one on the bread lines," Alex agreed.

I pulled up to the curb across the street from the Brattice place. It's a beautiful home. Light lemon yellow with dark green shutters. It reminds me a little of Cabot House. An immaculately manicured lawn leads up to a row of pillars and a small porch which, in turn, leads to the main entrance of the house. To the right, a flagstone path goes from a detached garage to a second entrance. As we were absorbing the sight, the main door burst open and a woman ran out, followed closely by a man. She stopped on the lawn and confronted him.

Sam said, "I smell trouble." He took the portable phone out of his pocket and poked some buttons. "If the trouble I smell arrives, dial 911 and hit 'send'." He handed the phone to me and showed me the "send" key.

The drama on the front lawn continued. The woman shrieked, "You dumbfuck, you couldn't leave well enough alone, could you?"

"Shut your face! That pissant would have blabbed and you know it."

"So disappear him, you idiot! But trying to make it look like the mob? You're a joke."

The man hauled off and smacked her.

A kid ran out of the house. He was brandishing a gun. "Don't you hit my mom, you motherfucker." He fired a shot in the general direction of the man.

Sam said, "Do the 911 thing. When they answer, give them the address and tell them there's a weapon involved." He jumped out of the car, turning only to tell Alex to stay put or he'd shoot him. I don't think Sam meant it.

As Sam ran toward the fray, a black car, coming from the north, cut him off and pulled up on the lawn. Two guys in dark suits jumped out of the car. They each took one of the man's arms, frog marched him to the car, and left with a screech of tires. I looked for the license plate. It was covered with mud. We were in the middle of a mini-drought. Where did they get mud?

I called 911 and followed Sam's instructions. I was informed that the police would be there immediately.

Sam was dealing with the woman, so Alex and I left the Mustang and went to the kid. Alex said, "Give me the gun, son. Your target's been removed." The kid handed over the weapon.

Sirens heralded the arrival of the Alexandria police. Two cops jumped out of the car. One of them, gun drawn, ran toward Alex. Alex dropped the kid's weapon and put his hands up.

The other cop joined Sam and the woman. I edged over to eavesdrop. Sam identified himself as the Bella Villa County Sheriff. As soon as Sam produced his identification and explained Alex and me, the cop hailed his partner and let it be known that Alex was one of the good guys.

Alex's cop, who was about to handcuff my husband, put the cuffs away, secured the gun and engaged Alex in serious conversation.

Meanwhile, Sam was explaining that we were driving by when the fracas erupted. As soon as the kid came out and fired the gun, Sam tried to intervene to the extent of stabilizing the scene, but the black car arrived before he could cross the street.

Sam noticed me listening. "Bea, did you get the license plate?"

"I tried, but it was covered with mud. It was a Lincoln Town Car."

The cop asked Sam if he knew who owned the house. Sam allowed that he did.

"And you just happened to drive by?"

"Well," said Sam, in his 'Mayberry's Andy Griffith' mode, "we *intended* to drive by the house, but we just *happened* to drive by when all this started."

Alex and the other cop drifted over. Alex had his arm around the kid's shoulder. Alex's cop asked, "Why did you intend to drive by?"

"Because we think these people are involved in a homicide that took place in your jurisdiction but involved activities that took place on Federal property located in my jurisdiction. Someone found Adam Brattice's bones. The Federal Lab identified them. I was just curious as to what his house looked like."

Sam's cop said, "You talking about the billionaire that went missing years ago?"

Sam nodded. "Yeah. He lived in this house. I think this is his wife and kid. Our Feds have a felony that's probably related."

He smiled at the two cops. "Now if you officers would take this lady, whom I believe is Mrs. Brattice...

"You *are* Mrs. Brattice?" She nodded.

"If you officers would take Mrs. Brattice with you, we will follow you in order to brief whoever you think should be briefed."

The two cops conferred. Finally Alex's cop said, "Something this high profile, I think we better go right to the Chief. I'll call it in to our Captain. If he doesn't agree, he'll divert us."

Mrs. Brattice and the kid rode with the cops. We trailed them.

"Did you notice," Alex remarked, "that with all that noise and hoop-la not a single neighbor came out to see what was going on?"

I sat in the back seat. Sam and Alex in front. That gave Sam a little more room to stretch his long legs. "You know," Sam said, "this will be the first time I've ever seen a real city police headquarters. You've seen my place. We've got about fifteen deputies, all masterful at handling domestic violence and auto accidents. Don't know what we'd have done if you guys at LIT hadn't helped us out the couple of times we got in over our heads.

"But this force? They've got maybe two hundred well trained, well armed officers. They don't sweat nine hundred buck mobile phones. Can't imagine what it would be like running this outfit." Sam thought a minute. "Don't think I'd like it."

The cops led us to police headquarters. We went through a pair of glass doors into an anteroom containing an information desk, a flight of stairs and an elevator. The sergeant behind the desk informed the cops that their captain had called in. The Chief was expecting us. The cops left. The elevator door opened and two other cops emerged. One of them escorted the Brattices up the stairs.

The other cop smiled at the rest of us. "Get in the elevator with me and I'll take you to our leader."

At the third floor, we got out of the elevator, walked through another anteroom, and into a long corridor. Secretaries and their desks lined one wall. Closed office doors lined the other. The Chief's office was at the end of the corridor. It was a large office. An I-Love-Me display of framed citations covered the wall on the left. The Chief's desk and a couch were on the right. The back wall consisted of a bank of windows that looked out on some woods. A conference table and chairs sat in the center of the room. A middle-sized man of about fifty, smiled a greeting. "I'm Chief Reddy. I understand you have a tale to tell."

We parked ourselves around the conference table. For the most part, Sam did the briefing. Alex and I interrupted occasionally to add color.

After a bit, a cop entered. Reddy stood up, excused himself, and conferred with him for a few minutes.

He returned to the table. "A couple of my men are interviewing the woman and the kid together. Not usual, but Captain Morris said that the guys who brought them in noticed that the kid kept interrupting his mother and straightening her out.

"Useful," said Sam.

Reddy chuckled. "Indeed. They're both talking. She's been Mirandized, but it'll take a while for the shock to wear off and she realizes she'd better get a lawyer.

"Do you know who the missing man is?"

Alex said, "We think it's Adam Brattice's brother, but we don't know for sure."

"Do you have any idea who grabbed him?"

We testified that we had never seen those men before. What we assumed was another story.

We were allowed to go home but Chief Reddy would appreciate it if we were to be available for further conversation.

Before we had even reached the highway, Sam's phone squawked. It was Chief Reddy. Mrs. Brattice confirmed all of our surmises. Howard had indeed killed Cody. He had also left a dead rat on our doorstep and locked me in the basement.

"For God's sake," asked Sam, "why did he do that?"

"According to Mrs. Brattice," Chief Reddy said, "it's because he's a dumbfuck."

EPILOGUE
May 31, 1993

It was almost ten when we finally got out of bed. The earlier part of the morning had been well spent.

Alex said, "The PTA has a breakfast tent set up. Should we make breakfast here or eat there?" Discussion ensued, followed by compromise. We'd have coffee at home (we didn't trust PTA coffee) but would eat in Bella Villa.

Daryl intercepted us as we passed his house. Grinning, he stuck his head into the convertible. "Vengeance," he said, "is the Lord's, but the Lord moves in mysterious ways."

"What happened?"

"Sandy told you about her rotten neighbors who had the little dog put down?

I affirmed that.

"Well, they got that Alsatian and the husband trained him and trained him and there was no question but that the dog was his and no one else's. He's real proud of that. Friday morning, he left for work and his wife, who doesn't go out to work, was left with the dog. She let him out of the house and into the yard and when she went to bring him back in, he growled and snapped at her. He finally herded her into a corner of the yard and wouldn't let her out. Every time she moved he bared his teeth. He kept her in that corner for hours She musta been terrified. I'm surprised she didn't faint.

The husband finally comes home, finds his wife and the beast in the yard, and calls the dog off.

"Junior said that the couple have been screaming at one another for the last two days. She's threatening to leave him if he doesn't get rid of the dog and from what Junior has overheard, he's told her to pack her bags."

Alex was laughing. "Gee," he said, "if it comes to divorce, I wonder who'll get custody of the dog."

We arrived in town, snuck the Mustang into the sheriff's lot, and found the breakfast tent set up on the Village Green. It was doing a brisk business. We got in line behind a frumpy woman who was engaged in acrimonious conversation with Midge Petrofsky. I had no qualms about listening in.

The frump was saying, "...and I don't think it's right to have those colored people to be part of the goings on."

Midge didn't answer.

The frump continued. "After all, would you want your daughter to marry one?"

Midge said, "I don't have a daughter."

"But if you did."

Midge responded, "I have a son and I love having Arthur teaching him to play the drums and sharing our dinner table."

"Well it isn't right inviting them into the town like that. Who knows what they'll do. They could violate our women. Or rob us. Or who knows what? I'm certainly not going to vote for Claude the next time he runs for mayor."

"Thank you," said Midge. "It would be good to have at least one "no" vote. The elections were getting boring." She paid for her breakfast and went off to look for a place to sit. The frump paid and went in another direction.

Alex and I had assembled breakfasts of rumbled eggs, bacon, and rolls. We paid the bill and looked for Midge. We joined her and a couple of the high school teachers.

Midge said, "You heard that?"

I nodded. "Who is that woman?"

"Charity Nesbitt."

The two school teachers groaned. One of them said, "She's Bella Villa's POW."

"She was a prisoner of war?" Alex was amazed.

"No," said the other teacher. "She's a Piece of Work."

Midge laughed. "She doesn't like anybody and doesn't approve of anything. I don't think she ever married. She was single when she moved here about twenty years ago. Got a job at the bank, so she probably doesn't have a criminal record. She's been a teller ever since. My guess is that her biggest problem is that she's never been laid."

We all laughed.

We bussed our dishes and moved on. Alex said, "I don't believe Midge said that."

I said, "I don't believe I heard that."

We walked over to the corner of Maine and Maple where the parade would begin. Chaos reigned. Since the Memorial Day Parade had been held for as long as anyone could remember, we assumed that things would be sorted out in time to start in good order. We went looking for Chuck who was scheduled to bring up the rear. Our timing was exquisite. He and the trio were putting the finishing touches on the float.

"Can we help?" Alex asked.

"Sure thing," said Willis.

Rats! I'd thought we'd got away clean.

Chuck said, "When the parade's over and I get the float back here, could you meet me in the museum? I'll get the Winner to the museum on the hand truck, but the t-t-trio will have to perform. Could you give us a hand with the installation so they can get to the stage sooner?"

I said, "Absolutely. Will we be able to see the concert?"

"No problem," Arthur said. "You run around front while we're warming up. Chuck can peek around the curtain. We won't draw the curtain until Chuck sees you waving."

Chuck called. "M-m-move it guys, we're getting ready. I've got to get my float out of the way."

The Village Green was three blocks long from north to south and two blocks wide east to west. The museum and the courthouse sat on the east side of the Green, city hall and the jail on the west side. The metal llama was a permanent installation situated a few yards closer to the museum than to City Hall. A miscellany of objects had been added for Memorial Day. The breakfast tent had been placed in front of City Hall. The tables and chairs would be re-used for the partakers of the pig roast, which was sizzling away, smelling delicious, at the north end of Green. On the south end, as far away from the fire as could be managed, was a bounce tent for the kids and a strength-o-meter for the big boys. My guess was that Arthur would demolish it. Sprinkled around the Green was an assortment of amusements including, but not limited to, a ring toss, a popcorn stand, and Madam LaZooka, the fortune teller, sitting on a golden chair under a canopy. She was swathed in a variety of shawls and wore bracelets up to her elbows. Her face was slathered with a barrel of pancake make-up, a boatload of rouge, and a mountain of blue eyeshadow. This artistic arrangement was topped by a jet black wig under a purple turban. She looked faintly familiar. I inspected her closely. It was Claudia Coker.

Buddy had set up a little stand to the right of Madam LaZooka. He was selling jams, jellies, and preserves from the kitchens of the locals. A sign announced that the proceeds would be donated to the Trio's Foundation. When we walked up, Buddy was in serious conversation with Young Daryl, who was trying to persuade him to open a grocery store near Oxford. We heard the words "great market" from Daryl and "overextended" from Buddy. They paused in the discussion long enough for Buddy to sell us a jar of hot pepper jelly.

The parade route was straightforward. It started on Main and Maple, one block north and one block east of the Green. It would go south on Maple to Green Street, one block from the southeast corner of the Green, turn right to Bella Villa Street on the southwest corner and then back to where it began.

Alex and I opted to watch on Maple near the back of the museum. This would make it easy to slip into the museum to help with the installation. Or so we thought. The area was packed. Not an inch to wiggle in. We were wondering what to do when we heard a shout. Dexter Hamilton, the manager of Cabot House waved to us. "Over here, we'll make room."

We squeezed through the crowd and discovered that almost the entire Cabot House staff was in attendance. They incorporated us just in time to see the arrival of The Volunteer Fire Department, bells clanging, siren whooping. Sam and the County Sheriff's Department followed. Sam blew us a kiss as they marched by. The deputies were followed by a baton twirler. She wasn't very good, so she had an assistant whose function was to retrieve errant baton tosses. Fortunately, none of the spectators had been brained. At least not yet. Then came the high school band. They were no more musical than in rehearsal, but who cared? After that came Mayor Petrofsky and the town council, waving from a little open-roofed bus. This was followed by a WW II Jeep in which sat some veterans of the war of the same name. It looked like their number had been depleted somewhat from last year. Younger guys from subsequent wars followed on foot. Then a flower-covered float from Cabot House and after that came the gussied-up town dogs, horses and riders, Boy and Girl Scouts, a line of tractors from the neighboring farms, and finally the float displaying this year's winner of the Stump Chuck contest as well as Chuck himself. He was waving majestically to the crowd.

As soon as Chuck's float passed, we bade farewell to the Cabot House crew amid mutual expressions of love and regard, and scooted into the museum where we awaited the arrival of the Winner. The main part of the museum was empty of people. We heard noises from the office but the door was firmly shut with a "No Admittance" sign affixed to it.

Alex and I amused ourselves by activating the various cubes and watching the displays strut their stuff. Finally, the back door opened and Chuck and the Winner appeared. The office door opened and the trio emerged. Arthur and Chuck hoisted and held the Winner while Lomas and Willis guided them to the vacant cube on the museum floor. Alex and I got the electrical wires out of the way. Arthur and Chuck gently lowered the Winner onto the cube. The three musicians then returned to the office. Alex, Chuck, and I turned our attention to improving the Winner's position, dusting the debris off of its several parts, and tending to the electrical connections. We gave it a trial run. Perfect.

Chuck mounted the steps to the stage while Alex and I wiggled through the left side curtain and took our places in the front row where Claude and Midge had made room for us. We gave the high sign to Chuck, who was peeping out the front curtain.

Shortly came the bum bum bum bum bum of the drum. The curtain parted and there were *We Three*, dressed in immaculate tuxes and standing close together. They parted and there sat Petey, also in a tux, plying his drumsticks. Midge and Claude both gasped. Apparently they hadn't been let in on the secret.

As the audience realized who was playing the drums, a cheer and wild applause broke out. Arthur nodded to Petey who stood up and made a dignified bow. He sat back down and took up his sticks.

Then Lomas, bowing the bass, began the Washington Post March. Willis entered on the sax. Petey kept up the background rhythm while Arthur tapped the cymbals when it was called for. I teared up. Looked at Alex. He also had teared up.

When the March ended, Petey left the stage and presently wormed his way to stand between Midge and Claude. "Mommy, Daddy was I good?"

"You were perfect, Pete." Midge gave him a hug.

"Don't go way. I got more to do." He looked at Alex and me. "Don't you go way either. The rest is really really good."

Arthur then began a slow beat on the kettle drum. Willis stepped forward and began an *a capella* version of Amazing Grace sung, Petey informed us, entirely in the Cherokee language. The audience was absolutely still. When he stepped back, for perhaps a full minute there was no reaction from the audience. Then a lone hand clap. Then thunderous applause. Willis bowed.[5]

Petey let go of Midge's hand and trotted off.

Next, *We Three* swung into a kooky version of the 1812 Overture. Bobby McFerrin why weren't you here to listen to this?

Finally, the trio began America the Beautiful.

Willis's baritone began: *O, beautiful for spacious skies,*

Then came a thrilling mezzo-soprano. Michelle mounted the stairs. I turned to Alex, "That's Arthur's wife."

For amber waves of grain,

Then a full-bodied contralto. "That's Glenna. She was at Chrissie's and my table." She joined Michelle.

For purple mountain majesties

A glorious soprano entered. All three women were in tuxes. "That's Florence Barney. She joined our table. She must have been responsible for the tuxes."

---

[5]*Amazing Grace* in the Cherokee language is on the 1996 Walella album

195

Above the fruited plain,
And rounding out the chorus – Petey.
He ran up the stairs and stationed himself between Florence and Glenna. They all held hands and sang.

America, America God shed his grace on thee,
Lomas beckoned the crowd to join them.
And crown thy good with brotherhood
From sea to shining sea.

THE END

GLOSSARY OF YIDDISH WORDS AND PHRASES USED IN THIS BOOK

bubeleh - darling, honey, sweetie

bubkes - absolutely nothing

gonif - a thief

gottenyu - Dear God!

kup - head

mentsh - an honorable, decent person

meshuggener - a crazy person

momser - a bastard in the same sense that "bastard" is used
      in English. A nogoodnik

nu - a general word that expects a reply. It can mean "Huh?",
      "So tell me", "What's going on?" and so on

paskudnik - a nasty, deceiving, low-life

putz - penis, in vulgar society, a nasty, petty, and small
      minded man

schmuck - a jerk, a contemptible person

shmegegge - a foolish dolt

shtunk - a rotten person

tokke - would you believe?

tsores - trouble

tuchas - buttocks, rear-end